P9-CRH-165

"Are you lonely, Harden?"

Miranda asked.

Harden drew in a slow breath. "Yes, I'm lonely," he said harshly. "I've never been any other way."

"Always on the outside looking in," she murmured. "Yes, I know how it feels."

Slowly, he raised a hand to her face and traced the firm, full curve of her mouth, watching her lips part and follow his finger helplessly. She reacted to him instantly. It made his head spin with delicious sensations.

She caught his wrist. "Please," she whispered. "Don't."

"Does it make you feel guilty to let me pleasure you?" he asked quietly. "It isn't something I offer very often."

"I guess I do feel guilty," she admitted.

He drew her to him and enveloped her in his hard arms, holding her while the tears fell. "Give yourself time." His lips brushed her temple. "Miranda, everyone has a secret shame, a searing guilt. It's part of being human. You can get through the pain if you just think past it. Think ahead. Find something to look forward to."

"Does it work?"

"It got me through my own rough time," he replied.

"Want to tell me what it was?"

He smiled at her gently. "No."

Dear Reader:

Welcome to Silhouette Romance—experience the magic of the wonderful world where two people fall in love. Meet heroines who will make you cheer for their happiness and heroes (be they the boy next door or a handsome, mysterious stranger) who will win your heart. Silhouette Romance novels reflect the magic of love—sweeping you away with stories that will make you laugh and cry; heartwarming, poignant stories that will move you time and time again.

In the next few months, we're publishing romances by many of your all-time favorites such as Diana Palmer, Brittany Young, Annette Broadrick and many others. Your response to these authors and other authors in Silhouette Romance has served as a touchstone for us, and we're pleased to bring you more books with Silhouette's distinctive medley of charm, wit and—above all—*romance*.

During 1991, we have many special events planned. Don't miss our WRITTEN IN THE STARS series. Each month in 1991, we're proud to present readers with a book that focuses on the hero—and his astrological sign.

I hope you'll enjoy this book and all of the stories to come. Come home to romance—Silhouette Romance—for always!

Sincerely,

Tara Gavin
Senior Editor

DIANA PALMER

Harden

Published by Silhouette Books New York

America's Publisher of Contemporary Romance

SILHOUETTE BOOKS
300 E. 42nd St., New York, N.Y. 10017

HARDEN

Copyright © 1991 by Diana Palmer

All rights reserved. Except for use in any review,
the reproduction or utilization of this work in
whole or in part in any form by any electronic,
mechanical or other means, now known or
hereafter invented, including xerography,
photocopying and recording, or in any information
storage or retrieval system, is forbidden without
the permission of Silhouette Books, 300 E. 42nd St.,
New York, N.Y. 10017

ISBN: 0-373-08783-7

First Silhouette Books printing March 1991

All the characters in this book are fictitious. Any
resemblance to actual persons, living or dead, is
purely coincidental.

®: Trademark used under license and
registered in the United States Patent and
Trademark Office and in other countries.

Printed in the U.S.A.

Books by Diana Palmer

Silhouette Romance

Darling Enemy #254
Roomful of Roses #301
Heart of Ice #314
Passion Flower #328
Soldier of Fortune #340
After the Music #406
Champagne Girl #436
Unlikely Lover #472
Woman Hater #532
*Calhoun #580
*Justin #592
*Tyler #604
*Sutton's Way #670
*Ethan #694
*Connal #741
*Harden #783

*Long, Tall Texans

Silhouette Special Edition

Heather's Song #33
The Australian #239

Silhouette Books

Silhouette Summer Sizzlers 1990
"Miss Greenhorn"
Silhouette Christmas Stories 1987
"The Humbug Man"

Silhouette Desire

The Cowboy and the Lady #12
September Morning #26
Friends and Lovers #50
Fire and Ice #80
Snow Kisses #102
Diamond Girl #110
The Rawhide Man #157
Lady Love #175
Cattleman's Choice #193
The Tender Stranger #230
Love by Proxy #252
Eye of the Tiger #271
Loveplay #289
Rawhide and Lace #306
Rage of Passion #325
Fit for a King #349
Betrayed by Love #391
Enamored #420
Reluctant Father #469
Hoodwinked #492
His Girl Friday #528
Hunter #606
Nelson's Brand #618

Also by Diana Palmer

Diana Palmer Duets Book I
Diana Palmer Duets Book II
Diana Palmer Duets Book III
Diana Palmer Duets Book IV
Diana Palmer Duets Book V
Diana Palmer Duets Book VI

DIANA PALMER

is a prolific romance writer who got her start as a newspaper reporter. Accustomed to the daily deadlines of a journalist, she has no problem with writer's block. In fact, she averages a book every two months. Mother of a young son, Diana met and married her husband within one week. "It was just like something from one of my books."

OKLAHOMA

NEW MEXICO

Dallas

Fort Worth ●

TEXAS

San Antonio ●

Houston ●

<u>Jacobsville</u>

Victoria ●

Gulf of Mexico

MEXICO

N

<u>Underlined</u> places are fictitious.

Chapter One

The bar wasn't crowded. Harden wished it had been, so that he could have blended in better. He was the only customer in boots and a Stetson, even if he was wearing an expensive gray suit with them. But the thing was, he stood out, and he didn't want to.

A beef producers' conference was being held at this uptown hotel in Chicago, where he'd booked a luxury suite for the duration. He was giving a workshop on an improved method of crossbreeding. Not that he'd wanted to; his brother Evan had volunteered him, and it had been too late to back out by the time Harden found out. Of his three brothers, Evan was the one he was closest to. Under the other man's good-natured kidding was a temper even hotter than Harden's and a ferocity of spirit that made him a keen ally.

Harden sipped his drink, feeling his aloneness keenly. He didn't fit in well with most people. Even his in-laws found him particularly disturbing as a dinner companion, and he knew it. Sometimes it was difficult just to get through the day. He felt incomplete; as if something crucial was missing in his life. He'd come down here to the lounge to get his mind off the emptiness. But he felt even more alone as he looked around him at the laughing, happy couples who filled the room.

His flinty pale blue eyes glittered at an older woman nearby making a play for a man. Same old story. Bored housewife, handsome stranger, a one-night fling. His own mother could have written a book on that subject. He was the result of her amorous fling, the only outsider in a family of four boys.

Everybody knew Harden was illegitimate. It didn't bother him so much anymore, but his hatred of the female sex, like his contempt for his mother, had never dwindled. And there was another reason, an even more painful one, why he could never forgive his mother. It was much more damning than the fact of his illegitimacy, and he pushed the thought of it to the back of his mind. Years had passed, but the memory still cut like a sharp knife. It was why he hadn't married. It was why he probably never would.

Two of his brothers were married. Donald, the youngest Tremayne, had succumbed four years ago. Connal had given in last year. Evan was still single. He and Harden were the only bachelors left. Theodora, their mother, did her best to throw eligible women at them. Evan enjoyed them. Harden did not. He had no use for women these days. At one time, he'd even considered becoming a minister. That had gone the way of most boyish dreams. He was a man now, and had his share of responsibility for the Tremayne ranch. Besides, he'd never really felt the calling for the cloth. Or for anything else.

A silvery laugh caught his attention and he glanced at the doorway. Despite his hostility toward anything in skirts, he couldn't tear his eyes away. She was beautiful. The most beautiful creature he'd ever seen in his life. She had long, wavy black hair halfway down her back. Her figure was exquisite, perfectly formed from the small thrust of her high breasts to the nipped-in waist of her silver cocktail dress. Her legs were encased in hose, and they were as perfect as the rest of her. He let his gaze slide back up to her creamy complexion with just the right touch of makeup, and he allowed himself to wonder what color her eyes were.

As if sensing his scrutiny, her head abruptly turned from the man with her, and he saw that her eyes matched her dress. They were the purest silver, and despite the smile and the happy expression, they were the saddest eyes he'd ever seen.

She seemed to find him as fascinating as he found her. She stared at him openly, her eyes lingering on his long, lean face with its pale blue eyes and jet-black hair and eyebrows. After a minute, she realized that she was staring and she averted her face.

They sat down at a table near him. The woman had obviously been drinking already, because she was loud.

"Isn't this fun?" she was saying. "Goodness, Sam, I never realized that alcohol tasted so nice! Tim never drank."

"You have to stop thinking about him," the other man said firmly. "Have some peanuts."

"I'm not an elephant," she said vehemently.

"Will you stop? Mindy, you might at least pretend that you're improving."

"I do. I pretend from morning until night, haven't you noticed?"

"Listen, I've got to—" There was a sudden beeping sound. The man muttered something and shut it off. "Damn the luck! I'll have to find a phone. I'll be right back, Mindy."

Mindy. The name suited her somehow. Harden twisted his shot glass in his hand as he studied her back and wondered what the nickname was short for.

She turned slightly, watching her companion dial a number at a pay phone. The happy expression went into eclipse and she looked almost desperate, her face drawn and somber.

Her companion, meanwhile, had finished his phone call and was checking his watch even as he rejoined her.

"Damn," he cursed again, "I've got a call. I'll have to go to the hospital right away. I'll drop you off on the way."

"No need, Sam," she replied. "I'll phone Joan and have her take me home. You go ahead."

"Are you sure you want to go back to the apartment? You know you're welcome to stay with me."

"I know. You've been very kind, but it's time I went back."

"You don't mind calling Joan?" he added reluctantly. "Your apartment is ten minutes out of my way, and every second counts in an emergency."

"Go!" she said. "Honest, I'm okay."

He grimaced. "All right. I'll phone you later."

He bent, but Harden noticed that he kissed her on the cheek, not the lips.

She watched him go with something bordering on relief. Odd reaction, Harden thought, for a woman who was obviously dating a man.

She turned abruptly and saw Harden watching her. With a sultry laugh she picked up the piña colada she'd ordered and got to her feet. She moved fluidly to Harden's table and without waiting for an invitation, she sat down, sprawling languidly in the chair across from him. Her gaze was as direct as his, curious and cautious.

"You've been staring at me," she said.

"You're beautiful," he returned without inflection. "A walking work of art. I expect everyone stares."

She lifted both elegant eyebrows, clearly surprised. "You're very forthright."

"Blunt," he corrected, lifting his glass in a cynical salute before he drained it. "I don't beat around the bush."

"Neither do I. Do you want me?"

He cocked his head, not surprised, even if he was oddly disappointed. "Excuse me?"

She swallowed. "Do you want to go to bed with me?" she asked.

His broad shoulders rose and fell. "Not particularly," he said simply. "But thanks for the offer."

"I wasn't offering," she replied. "I was going to tell you that I'm not that kind of woman. See?"

She proffered her left hand, displaying a wedding band and an engagement ring.

Harden felt a hot stirring inside him. She was married. Well, what had he expected? A beauty like that would be married, of course. And she was out with a man who wasn't her husband. Contempt kindled in his eyes.

"I see," he replied belatedly.

Mindy saw the contempt and it hurt. "Are you...married?" she persisted.

"Nobody brave enough for that job," he returned. His eyes narrowed and he smiled coldly. "I'm hell on the nerves, or so they tell me."

"A womanizer, you mean?"

He leaned forward, his pale blue eyes as cold as the ice they resembled. "A woman hater."

The way he said it made her skin chill. She rubbed warm hands over her upper arms. "Oh."

"Doesn't your husband mind you going out with other men?" he asked mockingly.

"My husband...died," she bit off the word. She took a sudden deep sip of her drink and then another, her brows drawn together. "Three weeks ago." Her face contorted suddenly. "I can't bear it!"

She got up and rushed out of the bar, her purse forgotten in her desperate haste.

Harden knew the look he'd just seen in her eyes. He knew the sound, as well. It brought him to his feet in an instant. He crammed her tiny purse into his pocket, paid for his drink, and went right out behind her.

It didn't take him long to find her. There was a bridge nearby, over the Chicago River. She was leaning over it, her posture stiff and suggestive as she held the rails.

Harden moved toward her with quick, hard strides, noticing her sudden shocked glance in his direction.

"Oh, hell, no, you don't," he said roughly and abruptly dragged her away from the rails. He shook her once, hard. "Pull yourself together, for God's sake! This is stupid!"

She seemed to realize then where she was. She looked at the water below and shivered. "I...wouldn't really have done it. I don't think I would," she stammered. "It's just that it's so hard, to go on. I can't eat, I can't sleep...!"

"Committing suicide isn't the answer," he said stubbornly.

Her eyes glittered like moonlit water in her tragic face as she looked up at him. "What is?"

"Life isn't perfect," he said. "Tonight, this minute, is all we really have. No yesterdays. No tomorrows. There's only the present. Everything else is a memory or a daydream."

She wiped her eyes with a beautifully manicured hand, her nails palest pink against her faintly tanned skin. "Today is pretty horrible."

"Put one foot forward at a time. Live from one minute to the next. You'll get through."

"Losing Tim was terrible enough, you see," she said, trying to explain. "But I was pregnant. I lost the baby in the accident, too. I was...I was driving." She looked up, her face terrible. "The road was slick and I lost control of the car. I killed him! I killed my baby and I killed Tim...!"

He took her by the shoulders, fascinated by the feel of her soft skin even as he registered the thinness of them. "God decided that it was his time to die," Harden corrected.

"There isn't a God!" she whispered, her face white with pain and remembered anguish.

"Yes, there is," he said softly. His broad chest rose and fell. "Come on."

"Where are you taking me?"

"Home."

"No!"

She was pulling against his hand. "I won't go back there tonight, I can't! He haunts me...."

He stopped. His eyes searched her face quietly. "I don't want you physically. But you can stay with me tonight, if you like. There's a spare bed and you'll be safe."

He couldn't believe he was making the offer. He, who hated women. But there was something so terribly fragile about her. She wasn't sober, and he didn't want her trying something stupid. It would lie heavily on his conscience; at least, that was what he told himself to justify his interest.

She stared at him quietly. "I'm a stranger."

"So am I."

She hesitated. "My name is Miranda Warren," she said finally.

"Harden Tremayne. You're not a stranger anymore. Come on."

She let him guide her back to the hotel, her steps not quite steady. She looked up at him curiously. He was wearing an expensive hat and suit. Even his boots looked expensive. Her mind was still whirling, but she had enough sense left to realize that he might think she was targeting him because he had money.

"I should go to my own apartment," she said hesitantly.

"Why?"

He was blunt. So was she. "Because you look very well-to-do. I'm a secretary. Tim was a reporter. I'm not at all wealthy, and I don't want you to get the wrong idea about me."

"I told you, I don't want a woman tonight," he said irritably.

"It isn't just that." She shifted restlessly. "You might think I deliberately staged all this to rob you."

His eyebrows rose. "What an intriguing thought," he murmured dryly.

"Yes, isn't it?" she said wryly. "But if I were planning any such thing, I'd pick someone who looked less dangerous."

He smiled faintly. "Afraid of me?" he asked deeply.

She searched his hard face. "I have a feeling I should be. But, no, I'm not. You've been very kind. I just had a moment's panic. I wouldn't really have thrown myself off the bridge, you know. I hate getting wet.'' She shifted. "I really should go home."

"You really should come with me," he replied. "I won't rest, wondering if you've got another bridge picked out. Come on. I don't think you're a would-be thief, and I'm tired."

"Are you sure?" she asked.

He nodded. "I'm sure."

She let him lead her into the hotel and around to the elevator. It was one of the best hotels in the city, and he went straight up to the luxury suites. He unlocked the door and let her in. There was a huge sitting room that led off in either direction to two separate bedrooms. Evan had planned to come up with Harden from Texas. At the last minute, though, there'd been an emergency and Evan had stayed behind to handle it.

Miranda began to feel nervous. She really knew nothing about this man, and she knew she was out of control. But there was something in his eyes that reassured her. He was a strong man. He positively radiated strength, and she needed that tonight. Needed someone to lean on, someone to take care of her, just this once. Tim had been more child than husband, always expecting her to handle things. Bills, telephone calls about broken appliances, the checkbook, groceries, dry cleaning, housekeeping—all that had been Miranda's job. Tim worked and came home and watched television, and then expected sex on demand. Miranda hadn't liked sex. It was an unpleasant duty that she tried to perform with the same resignation that she applied to all her other chores.

Tim knew, of course he did. She'd gotten pregnant, and Tim hadn't liked it. He found her repulsive pregnant. That had been an unexpected benefit. But now there was no pregnancy. Her hand went to her stomach and her face contorted. She'd lost her baby....

"Stop that," Harden said unexpectedly, his pale blue eyes flashing at her when he saw the expression on her face. "Agonizing over it isn't going to change one damned thing." He tossed his hotel key on the coffee table and motioned her into a chair. "I keep a pot of coffee on. Would you like a cup?"

"Yes, please," she said with resignation. She slumped down into the chair, feeling as if all the life had drained out of her. "I can get it," she added quickly, starting to rise.

He frowned. "I'm perfectly capable of pouring coffee," he said shortly.

"Sorry," she said with a shy smile. "I'm used to waiting on Tim."

He searched her eyes. "Had you trained, did he?" he asked.

She gasped.

He turned. "Black, or do you like something in it?"

"I...I like it black," she stammered.

"Good. There's no cream."

She'd never been in a hotel penthouse before. It was beautiful. It overlooked the lake and the beachfront, and she didn't like thinking about what it must have cost. She got to her feet and walked a little unsteadily to the patio door that overlooked Chicago at night. She wanted to go outside and get a breath of air, but she couldn't get the sliding door to work.

"Oh, for God's sake, not again!" came a curt, angry deep voice from behind her. Lean, strong hands caught her waist from behind, lifting and turning her effortlessly before he frog-marched her back to her chair and sat her down in it. "Now stay put," he said shortly. "I am not having any more leaping episodes tonight, do you understand me?"

She swallowed. He was very tall, and extremely intimidating. She'd always managed to manipulate Tim when he had bad moods, but this man didn't look as if he was controllable any way at all. "Yes," she said through tight lips. "But I wasn't going to jump. I just wanted to see the view—"

He cut her off. "Here. Drink this. It won't sober you up, but it might lighten your mood a bit."

He pushed a cup and saucer toward her. The smell of strong coffee drifted up into her nostrils as she lifted the cup.

"Careful," he said. "Don't spill it on that pretty dress."

"It's old," she replied with a sad smile. "My clothes have to last years. Tim was furious that I wasted money on this one, but I wanted just one nice dress."

He sat down across from her and leaned back, crossing his long legs before he lit a cigarette and dragged an ashtray closer. "If you don't like the smoke, I'll turn the air conditioning up," he offered.

"I don't mind it," she replied. "I used to smoke, but Tim made me quit. He didn't like it."

Harden was getting a picture of the late Tim that *he* didn't like. He blew out a cloud of smoke, his eyes raking her face, absorbing the fragility in it. "What kind of secretary are you?"

"Legal," she said. "I work for a firm of attorneys. It's a good job. I'm a paralegal now. I took night courses to learn it. I do a lot of legwork and researching along with typing up briefs and such. It gives me some freedom, because I'm not chained to a desk all day."

"The man you were with tonight..."

"Sam?" She laughed. "It isn't like that. Sam is my brother."

His eyebrows arched. "Your brother takes you on drinking sprees?"

"Sam is a doctor, and he hardly drinks at all. He and Joan—my sister-in-law—have been letting me stay with them since...since the accident. But tonight I was going home. I'd just come from an office party. I certainly didn't feel like a party, but I got dragged in because everyone thought a few drinks might make me feel better. They did. But one of my co-workers thought I was feeling too much better so she called Sam to come and get me. Then I wanted to come here and try a piña colada and Sam humored me because I threatened to make a scene." She smiled. "Sam is very straitlaced. He's a surgeon."

"You don't favor each other."

She laughed, and it was like silvery bells all over again. "He looks like our father. I look like our mother's mother. There are just the two of us. Our parents were middle-aged when they married and had us. They died within six months of each other when

Sam was still in medical school. He's ten years older than I am, you see. He practically raised me.''

"His wife didn't mind?''

"Oh, no,'' she said, remembering Joan's kindness and maternal instincts. "They can't have children of their own. Joan always said I was more like her daughter than her sister-in-law. She's been very good to me.''

He couldn't imagine anybody not being good to her. She wasn't like the women he'd known in the past. This one seemed to have a heart. And despite her widowed status, there was something very innocent about her, almost naive.

"You said your husband was a reporter,'' he said when he'd finished his coffee.

She nodded. "He did sports. Football, mostly.'' She smiled apologetically. "I hate football.''

He chuckled faintly and took another draw from his cigarette. "So do I.''

Her eyes widened. "Really? I thought all men loved it.''

He shook his head. "I like baseball.''

"I don't mind that,'' she agreed. "At least I understand the rules.'' She sipped her coffee and studied him over the rim of the cup. "What do you do, Mr. Tremayne?''

"Harden,'' he corrected. "I buy and sell cattle. My brothers and I own a ranch down in Jacobsville, Texas.''

"How many brothers do you have?''

"Three.'' The question made him uncomfortable. They weren't really his brothers, they were his half brothers, but he didn't want to get into specifics like that. Not now. He turned his wrist and glanced at his thin gold watch. "It's midnight. We'd better call it a day. There's a spare bedroom through there," he indicated with a careless hand. "And a lock on the door, if it makes you feel more secure."

She shook her head, her gentle eyes searching his hard face. "I'm not afraid of you," she said quietly. "You've been very kind. I hope that someday, someone is kind to you when you need help."

His pale eyes narrowed, glittered. "I'm not likely to need it, and I don't want thanks. Go to bed, Cinderella."

She stood up, feeling lost. "Good night, then."

He only nodded, busy crushing out his cigarette. "Oh. By the way, you left this behind." He pulled her tiny purse from his jacket pocket and tossed it to her.

Her purse! In her desperate flight, she'd forgotten all about it. "Thank you," she said.

"No problem. Good night." He added that last bit very firmly and she didn't stop to argue.

She went quickly into the bedroom—it was almost as large as the whole of the little house she lived in—and she quietly closed the door. She didn't have anything to sleep in except her slip, but that wouldn't matter. She was tired to death.

It wasn't until she was almost asleep that she remembered nobody would know where she was. She hadn't called Joan to come and get her, as she'd promised Sam she would, and she hadn't phoned her brother to leave any message. Well, nobody would miss her for a few hours, she was sure. She closed her eyes and let herself drift off to sleep. For the first time since the accident, she slept soundly, and without nightmares.

Chapter Two

Miranda awoke slowly, the sunlight pouring in through the wispy curtains and drifting across her sleepy face. She stretched lazily and her eyes opened. She frowned. She was in a strange room. She sat up in her nylon slip and stared around her, vaguely aware of a nagging ache in her head. She put a hand to it, pushing back her disheveled dark hair as her memory began to filter through her confused thoughts.

She got up quickly and pulled her dress over her head, zipping it even as she stepped into her shoes and looked around for her purse. The clock on the bed-side table said eight o'clock and she was due at work in thirty minutes. She groaned. She'd never make it. She had to get a cab and get back to her apartment, change and fix her makeup—she was going to be late!

She opened the door and exploded into the sitting room to find Harden in jeans and a yellow designer T-shirt, just lifting the lid off what smelled like bacon and eggs.

"Just in time," he mused, glancing at her. "Sit down and have something to eat."

"Oh, I can't," she wailed. "I have to be at work at eight-thirty, and I still have to get to my apartment and change, and look at me! People will stare...!"

He calmly lifted the telephone receiver and handed it to her. "Call your office and tell them you've got a headache and you won't be in until noon."

"They'll fire me!" she wailed.

"They won't. Dial!"

She did, automatically. He had that kind of abrasive masculinity that seemed to dominate without conscious effort, and she responded to it as she imagined most other people did. She got Dee at the office and explained the headache. Dee laughed, murmuring something about there being a lot of tardiness that morning because of the office party the night before. They'd expect her at noon, she added and hung up.

"Nobody was surprised," she said, staring blankly at the phone.

"Office parties wreak havoc," he agreed. "Call your brother so he won't worry about you."

She hesitated.

"Something wrong?" he asked.

"What do I tell him?" she asked worriedly, nibbling her lower lip. "'Hi, Sam, I've just spent the night with a total stranger'?"

He chuckled softly. "That wasn't what I had in mind."

She shook her head. "I'll think of something as I go." She dialed Sam's home number and got him instead of Joan. "Sam?"

"Where the devil are you?" her brother raged.

"I'm at the Carlton Arms," she said. "Look, I'm late for work and it's a long story. I'll tell you everything later, I promise..."

"You'll damned well tell me everything now!"

Harden held out his hand and she put the phone into it, aware of the mocking, amused look on his hard face.

She moved toward the breakfast trolley, absently aware of the abrupt, quiet explanation he was giving her brother. She wondered if he was always so cool and in control, and reasoned that he probably was. She lifted the lid off one of the dishes and sniffed the delicious bacon. He'd ordered breakfast for two, and she was aware of a needling hunger.

"He wants to talk to you," Harden said, holding out the phone.

She took it. "Sam?" she began hesitantly.

"It's all right," he replied, pacified. "You're apparently in good hands. Just pure luck, of course," he added angrily. "You can't pull a stunt like that again. I'll have a heart attack."

"I won't. I promise," she said. "No more office parties. I'm off them for life."

"Good. Call me tonight."

"I will. Bye."

She hung up and smiled at Harden. "Thanks."

He shrugged. "Sit down and eat. I've got a workshop at eleven for the cattlemen's conference. I'll drop you off at your place first."

She vaguely remembered the sign she'd seen on the way into the hotel about a beef producers seminar. "Isn't the conference here?" she stammered.

"Sure. But I'll drop you off anyway."

"I don't know quite how to thank you," she began, her silver eyes soft and shy.

He searched her face for a long, long moment before he was able to drag his eyes back to his plate. "I don't care much for women, Miranda," he said tersely, "So call this a momentary aberration. But next time, don't put yourself in that kind of vulnerable situation. I didn't take advantage. Most other men would have."

She knew that already. She poured herself a cup of coffee from the carafe, darting curious glances at him. "Why don't you like women?"

His dark eyebrows clashed and he stared at her with hard eyes.

"It won't do any good to glower at me," she said gently. "I'm not intimidated. Won't you tell me?"

He laughed without humor. "Brave this morning, aren't we?"

"I'm sober," she replied. "And you shouldn't carry people home with you if you don't want them to ask questions."

"I'll remember that next time," he assured her as he lifted his fork.

"Why?" she persisted.

"I'm illegitimate."

She didn't flinch or look shocked. She sipped her coffee. "Your mother wasn't married to your father." She nodded.

He scowled. "My mother had a flaming affair and I was the result. Her husband took her back. I have three brothers who are her husband's children. I'm not."

"Was your stepfather cruel to you?" she asked gently.

He shifted restlessly. "No," he said reluctantly.

"Were you treated differently from the other boys?"

"No. Look," he said irritably, "why don't you eat your breakfast?"

"Doesn't your mother love you?"

"Yes, my mother loves me!"

"No need to shout, Mr. Tremayne." She grimaced, holding one ear. "I have perfect hearing."

"What business of yours is my life?" he demanded.

"You saved mine," she reminded him. "Now you're responsible for me for the rest of yours."

"I am not," he said icily.

She wondered at her own courage, because he looked much more intimidating in the light than he had the night before. He made her feel alive and safe and cosseted. Ordinarily she was a spirited, independent woman, but the trauma of the accident and the loss of the baby had wrung the spirit out of her. Now it was beginning to come back. All because of this tall, angry stranger who'd jerked her from what he'd thought were the waiting jaws of death. Actually jumping had been the very last thing in her mind on that bridge last night. It had been nausea that had her hanging over it, but it had passed by the time he reached her.

"Are you always so hard to get along with?" she asked pleasantly.

His pale blue eyes narrowed. Of course he was, but he didn't like hearing it from her. She confused him. He turned back to his food. "You'd better eat."

"The sooner I finish, the sooner I'm out of your hair?" she mused.

"Right."

She shrugged and finished her breakfast, washing it down with the last of her coffee. She didn't want to go. Odd, when he was so obviously impatient to be rid of her. He was like a security blanket that she'd just found, and already she was losing it. He gave her peace, made her feel whole again. The thought of being without him made her panicky.

Harden was feeling something similar. He, who'd sworn that never again would he give his heart, was experiencing a protective instinct he hadn't been aware he had. He didn't understand what was happening to him. He didn't like it, either.

"If you're finished, we'll go," he said tersely, rising to dig into his pocket for his car keys.

She left the last sip of coffee in the immaculate china cup and got to her feet, retrieving her small purse from the couch. She probably looked like a shipwreck survivor, she thought as she followed him to the door, and God knew what people would think when they saw her come downstairs in the clothes she'd worn the night before. How ridiculous, she chided herself. They'd think the obvious thing, of course. That she'd slept with him. She flushed as they went down in the elevator, hoping that he wouldn't see the expression on her face.

He didn't. He was much too busy cursing himself for being in that bar the night before. The elevator stopped and he stood aside to let her out.

It was unfortunate that his brother Evan had decided to fly up early for the workshop Harden was conducting on new beef production methods. It was even more unfortunate that Evan should be standing in front of the elevator when Harden and Miranda got off it.

"Oh, God," Harden ground out.

Evan's brown eyebrows went straight up and his dark eyes threatened to pop. "Harden?" he asked, leaning forward as if he wasn't really sure that this was his half brother.

Harden's blue eyes narrowed threateningly, and a dark flush spread over his cheekbones. Instinctively he took Miranda's arm.

"Excuse me. We're late," he told Evan, his eyes threatening all kinds of retribution.

Evan grinned, white teeth in a swarthy face flashing mischievously. "You aren't going to introduce me?" he asked.

"I'm Miranda Warren," Miranda said gently, smiling at him over Harden's arm.

"I'm Evan Tremayne," he replied. "Nice to meet you."

"Go home," Harden told Evan curtly.

"I will not," Evan said indignantly, towering over both of them. "I came to hear you tell people how to make more money raising beef."

"You heard me at the supper table last month—just before you volunteered me for this damned workshop!" he reminded the other man. "Why did you have to come to Chicago to hear it again?"

"I like Chicago." He pursed his lips, smiling appreciatively at Miranda. "Lots of pretty girls up here."

"This one is off-limits, so go away," Harden told him.

"He hates women," Evan told Miranda. "He doesn't even go on dates back home. What did you do, if you don't mind saying? I mean, you didn't drug him or hit him with some zombie spell . . . ?"

Miranda shifted closer to Harden involuntarily and slid a shy hand into his. Evan's knowing look made her feel self-conscious and embarrassed. "Actually—" she began reluctantly.

Harden cut her off. "She had a small problem last night, and I rescued her. Now I'm taking her home," he said, daring his brother to ask another question. "I'll see you at the workshop."

"You're all right?" Evan asked Miranda, with sincere concern.

"Yes." She forced a smile. "I've been a lot of trouble to Mr. Tremayne. I . . . really do have to go."

Harden locked his fingers closer into hers and walked past Evan without another word.

"Your brother is very big, isn't he?" Miranda asked, tingling all over at the delicious contact with

Harden's strong fingers. She wondered if he was even aware of holding her hand so tightly.

"Evan's a giant," he agreed. "The biggest of us all. Short on tact, sometimes."

"Look who's talking," she couldn't resist replying.

He glared down at her and tightened his fingers. "Watch it."

She smiled, sighing as they reached his car in the garage. "I don't guess I'll see you again?" she asked.

"Not much reason to, if you don't try jumping off bridges anymore," he replied, putting up a cool front. Actually he didn't like the thought of not seeing her again. But she was mourning a husband and baby and he didn't want involvement. It would be for the best if he didn't start anything. He was still wearing the scars from the one time he'd become totally involved.

"I had too much to drink," she said after he'd put her in the luxury car he'd rented at the airport the day before and climbed in beside her to start the engine. "I don't drink as a rule. That last piña colada was fatal."

"Almost literally," he agreed, glancing at her irritably. "Find something to occupy your mind. It will help get you through the rough times."

"I know." She looked down at her lap. "I guess your brother thinks I slept with you."

"Does it matter what people think?"

She looked over at him. "Not to you, I expect. But I'm disgustingly conventional. I don't even jaywalk."

"I'll square it with Evan."

"Thank you." She twisted her purse and stared out the window, her sad eyes shadowed.

"How long has it been?"

She sighed softly. "Almost a month. I should be used to it by now, shouldn't I?"

"It takes a year, they say, to completely get over a loss. We all mourned my stepfather for at least that long."

"Your name is Tremayne, like your brother's."

"And you wonder why? My stepfather legally adopted me. Only a very few people know about my background. It isn't obvious until you see me next to my half brothers. They're all dark-eyed."

"My mother was a redhead with green eyes and my father was blond and blue-eyed," she remarked. "I'm dark-haired and gray-eyed, and everybody thought I was adopted."

"You aren't?"

She smiled. "I'm the image of my mother's mother. She was pretty, of course..."

"What do you think you are, the Witch of Endor?" he asked on a hard laugh. He glanced at her while they stopped for a traffic light. "My God, you're devastating. Didn't anyone ever tell you?"

"Well, no," she stammered.

"Not even your husband?"

"He liked fair women with voluptuous figures," she blurted out.

"Then he should have married one," he said shortly. "There's nothing wrong with you."

"I'm flat chested," she said without thinking.

Which was a mistake, because he immediately glanced down at her bodice with a raised eyebrow that spoke volumes. "Somebody ought to tell you that men have varied tastes in women. There are a few who prefer women without massive... bosoms," he murmured when he saw her expression. "And you aren't flat-chested."

She swallowed. He made her feel naked. She folded her arms over her chest and stared out the window again.

"How long were you married?" he asked.

"Well... four months," she confessed.

"Happily?"

"I don't know. He seemed so different before we married. And then I got pregnant and he was furious. But I wanted a baby so badly." She had to take a breath before she could go on. "I'm twenty-five. He was the first man who ever proposed to me."

"I can't believe that."

"Well, I didn't always look like this," she said. "I'm nearsighted. I wear contact lenses now. I took a modeling course and learned how to make the most of what I had. I guess it worked, because I met Tim at the courthouse while I was researching and he asked me out that same night. We only went together two weeks before we got married. I didn't know him, I guess."

"Was he your first man?"

She gasped. "You're very blunt!"

"You know that already." He lit a cigarette while he drove. "Answer me."

"Yes," she muttered, glaring at him. "But it's none of your business."

"Any particular reason why you waited until marriage?"

The glare got worse. "I'm old-fashioned and I go to church!"

He smiled. It was a genuine smile, for once, too. "So do I."

"You?"

"Never judge a book by its cover," he murmured. His pale eyes glanced sideways and he laughed.

She shook her head. "Miracles happen every day, they say."

"Thanks a lot." He stopped at another red light. "Which way from here?"

She gave him directions and minutes later, he pulled up in front of the small apartment house where she lived. It was in a fairly old neighborhood, but not a bad one. The house wasn't fancy, but it was clean and the small yard had flowers.

"There are just three apartments," she said. "One upstairs and two downstairs. I planted the flowers. This is where I lived before I married Tim. When he...died, Sam and Joan insisted that I stay with them. It's still hard to go in there. I did a stupid thing and bought baby furniture—" She stopped, swallowing hard.

He cut off the engine and got out, opening the door. "Come on. I'll go in with you."

He took her arm and guided her to the door, waiting impatiently while she unlocked it. "Do you have a landlady or landlord?"

"Absentee," she told him. "And I don't have a morals clause," she added, indicating her evening gown. "Good thing, I guess."

"You aren't a fallen woman," he reminded her.

"I know." She unlocked the door and let him in. The apartment was just as she'd left it, neat and clean. But there was a bassinet in one corner of the bedroom and a playpen in its box still sitting against the dividing counter between the kitchen and the dining room. She fought down a sob.

"Come here, little one," he said gently, and pulled her into his arms.

She was rigid at first, until her body adjusted to being held, to the strength and scent of him. He was very strong. She could feel the hard press of muscle against her breasts and her long legs. He probably did a lot of physical work around his ranch, because he was certainly fit. But his strength wasn't affecting her nearly as much as the feel of his big, lean hands against her back, and the warmth of his arms around her. He smelled of delicious masculine cologne and tobacco, and her lower body felt like molten liquid all of a sudden.

His fingers moved into the hair at her nape and their tips gently massaged her scalp. She felt his warm breath at her temple while he held her.

Tears rolled down her cheeks. She hadn't really cried since the accident. She made up for it now, pressing close to him innocently for comfort.

But the movement had an unexpected consequence, and she felt it against her belly. She stiffened and moved her hips demurely back from his with what she hoped was subtlety. All the same, her face flamed with embarrassment. Four brief months of marriage hadn't loosened many of her inhibitions.

Harden felt equally uncomfortable. His blood had cooled somewhat with age, and he didn't have much to do with women. His reaction to Miranda shocked and embarrassed him. Her reaction only made it worse, because when he lifted his head, he could see the scarlet blush on her face.

"Thanks again for looking after me last night," she said to ease the painful silence. Her hands slid around to his broad chest and rested there while she looked up into pale, quiet eyes in a face like stone. "I won't see you again?" she asked.

He shook his head. "It wouldn't be wise."

"I suppose not." She reached up hesitantly and touched his beautiful mouth, her fingertips lingering on the full, wide lower lip. "Thank you for my life," she said softly. "I'll take better care of it from now on."

"See that you do." He caught her fingers. "Don't do that," he said irritably, letting her hand fall to her side. He moved back, away from her. "I have to go."

"Yes, well, I won't keep you," she managed, embarrassed all over again. She hadn't meant to be so forward, but she'd never felt as secure with anyone before. It amazed her that such a sweeping emotion wouldn't be mutual. But he didn't look as if he even liked her, much less was affected by her. Except for that one telltale sign . . .

She went with him to the door and stood framed in the opening when he went out onto the porch.

He turned, his eyes narrow and angry as he gazed down at her. She looked vulnerable and sad and so alone. He let out a harsh breath.

"I'll be all right, you know," she said with false pride.

"Will you?" He moved closer, his stance arrogant, his eyes hot with feeling. His body throbbed as he looked at her. His gaze slid to her mouth and he couldn't help himself. He wanted it until it was an obsession. Reluctantly he caught the back of her neck in his lean hand and tilted her face as he bent toward her.

Her heart ran wild. She'd wanted his kiss so much, and it was happening. "Harden," she whispered helplessly.

"This is stupid," he breathed, but his mouth was already on hers even as he said it, the words going past her parted lips along with his smoky breath.

She didn't even hesitate. She slid her arms up around his neck and locked her hands behind his head, lifting herself closer to his hard, rough mouth. She moaned faintly, because the passion he kindled in her was something she'd never felt. Her legs trembled against his and she felt the shudder that buffeted him as his body reacted helplessly to her response.

He felt it and moved back. He dragged his mouth away from hers, breathing roughly as he looked down into her dazed eyes. "For God's sake!" he groaned.

He pushed her back into the apartment and followed her, elbowing the door shut before he reached for her again.

He wasn't even lucid. He knew he wasn't. But her mouth was the sweetest honey he'd ever tasted, and he didn't seem capable of giving it up.

She seemed equally helpless. Her body clung to his, her mouth protesting when he started to lift his. He sighed softly, giving in to her hunger, his mouth gentling as the kiss grew longer, more insistent. He toyed with her lips, teasing them into parting for him before his tongue eased gently past her teeth.

He felt her gasp even as he heard it. His hand smoothed her cheek, his thumb tenderly touching the corner of her mouth while his lips brushed it, calming her. She trembled. He persisted until she finally gave in, all at once, her soft body almost collapsing against him. His tongue pushed completely into her mouth and she shivered with passion.

The slow, rhythmic thrust of his tongue was so suggestive, so blatantly sexual, that it completely disarmed her. She hadn't expected this from a man she'd only met the day before. She hadn't expected her headlong reaction to him, either. She couldn't seem to let go, to draw back, to protest this fierce intimacy.

She moaned. The sound penetrated his mind, aroused him even more. He felt her legs trembling against his blatant arousal, and he forced his mouth to lift, his hands to clasp her waist and hold her roughly away from him while he fought for control of his senses.

Her face was flushed, her eyes half closed, drowsy with pleasure. Her soft mouth was swollen, still lifted, willing, waiting.

He shook her gently. "Stop it," he said huskily. "Or I'll have you right here, standing up."

She stared up at him only half comprehending, her breath jerking out of her tight throat, her heart slamming at her ribs. "What...happened?" she whispered.

He let go of her and stepped back, his face rigid with unsatisfied desire. His chest heaved with the force of his breathing. "God knows," he said tersely.

"I've...I've *never*..." she began, flustered with embarrassment.

"Oh, hell, I've 'never,' either," he said irritably. "Not like that." He had to fight for breath. He stared at her, fascinated. "That can't happen again. Ever."

She swallowed. She'd known that, too, but there had been a tiny hope that this was the beginning of something. Impossible, of course. She was a widow of barely one month, with emotional scars from the loss of her husband and child, and he was a man who obviously didn't want to get involved. Wrong time, wrong place, she thought sadly, and wondered how she was going to cope with this new hurt. "Yes. I know," she said finally.

"Goodbye, Miranda."

Her eyes locked with his. "Goodbye, Harden."

He turned with cold reluctance and opened the door again. He could still taste her on his mouth, and his body was taut with arousal. He paused with the doorknob in his hand. He couldn't make himself turn it. His spine straightened.

"It's too soon for you."

"I...suppose so."

There had been a definite hesitation there. He turned and looked at her, his eyes intent, searching.

"You're a city girl."

That wasn't quite true, but he obviously wanted to believe it. "Yes," she said.

He took a slow, steadying breath, letting his eyes run down her body before he dragged them back up to her face.

"Wrong time, wrong place," he said huskily.

She nodded. "Yes. I was thinking that, too."

So she was already reading his mind. This was one dangerous woman. It was a good thing that the timing was wrong. She could have tied him up like a trussed turkey.

His gaze fell to her flat belly and it took all his willpower not to think what sprang to his mind. He'd never wanted a child. Before.

"I'll be late for the workshop. And you'll be late for work. Take care of yourself," he said.

She smiled gently. "You, too. Thank you, Harden."

His broad shoulders rose and fell. "I'd have done the same for anyone," he said, almost defensively.

"I know that, too. So long."

He opened the door this time and went through it, without haste but without lingering. When he was back in the car, he forced himself to ignore the way it wounded him to leave her there alone with her painful memories.

Chapter Three

Evan was waiting for Harden the minute he walked into the hotel. Harden glowered at him, but it didn't slow the other man down.

"It's not my fault," Evan said as they walked toward the conference rooms where the workshop was to be held. "A venomous woman hater who comes downstairs with a woman in an evening gown at eight-thirty in the morning is bound to attract unwanted attention."

"No doubt." Harden kept walking.

Evan sighed heavily. "You never date anybody. You're forever on the job. My God, just seeing you with a woman is extraordinary. Tell me how you met her."

"She was leaning off a bridge. I stopped her."

"And...?"

Harden shrugged. "I let her use the spare room until she sobered up. This morning I took her home. End of story."

Evan threw up his hands. "Will you talk to me? Why was a gorgeous girl like that jumping off a bridge?"

"She lost her husband and a baby in a car accident," he replied.

Evan stopped, his eyes quiet and somber. "I'm sorry. She's still healing, is that it?"

"In a nutshell."

"So it was just compassion then." Evan shook his head and stuck his big hands into his pockets. "I might have known." He glanced at his half brother narrowly. "If you'd get married, I might have a chance of getting my own girl. They all walk over me trying to get to you. And you can't stand women." He brightened. "Maybe that's the secret. Maybe if I pretend to hate them, they'll climb all over me!"

"Why don't you try that?" Harden agreed.

"I have. It scared the last one off. No great loss. She had two cats and a hamster. I'm allergic to fur."

Harden laughed shortly. "So we've all noticed."

"I had a call from Mother earlier."

Harden's face froze. "Did you?"

"I wish you wouldn't do that," his brother said. "She's paid enough for what she did, Harden. You just don't understand how it is to be obsessively in love. Maybe that's why you've never forgiven her."

Evan had been away at college during the worst months of Harden's life. Neither Harden nor Theodora had ever told him much about the tragedy that had turned Harden cold. "Love is for idiots," Harden said, refusing to let himself remember. He paused to light a cigarette, his fingers steady and sure. "I want no part of it."

"Too bad," Evan replied. "It might limber you up a bit."

"Not much hope of that, at my age." He blew out a cloud of smoke, part of his mind still on Miranda and the way it had felt to kiss her. He turned toward the conference room. "I still don't understand why you came up here."

"To get away from Connal," he said shortly. "My God, he's driving me crazy."

Harden lifted an amused eyebrow. "Baby fever. Once Pepi gives birth, he'll be back to normal."

"He paces, he smokes, he worries about something going wrong. What if they don't recognize labor in time, what if the car won't start when it's time to go to the hospital!" He threw up his hands. "It's enough to put a man off fatherhood."

Fatherhood. Harden remembered looking hungrily at Miranda's waist and wondering how it would feel to father a child. Incredible thought, and he'd never had it before in his life, not even with the one woman he'd loved beyond bearing...or thought he'd loved. He scowled.

He had a lot of new thoughts and feelings with Miranda. This wouldn't do. They were strangers. He lived in Texas, she lived in Illinois. There was no future in it, even if she wasn't still in mourning. He had to bite back a groan.

"Something's eating you up," Evan said percep-
tively, narrowing one dark eye. "You never talk about
things that bother you."

"What's the use? They won't go away."

"No, but bringing them out in the light helps to get
them into perspective." He pursed his lips. "It's that
woman, isn't it? You saved her, now you feel responsible for her."

Harden whirled, his pale blue eyes glaring furiously
at the other man.

Evan held up both hands, grinning. "Okay, I get the
message. She was a dish, though. You might try your
luck. Donald and Connal and I can talk you through
a date...and the other things you don't know about."

Harden sighed. "Will you stop?"

"It's no crime to be innocent, even if you are a
man," Evan continued. "We all know you thought
about becoming a minister."

Harden just shook his head and kept walking.
Surely to God, Evan was a case. That assumption irritated him, but he wouldn't lower himself enough to
deny it.

"No comment?" Evan asked.

"No comment," Harden said pleasantly. "Let's go.
The crowd's already gathering."

Despite Harden's preoccupation with Miranda, the
workshop went well. He had a dry wit, which he used
to his advantage to keep the audience's attention while
he lectured on the combinations of maternal and car-
cass breeds that had been so successful back home.
Profit was the bottom line in any cattle operation, and

the strains he was using in a limited crossbreeding had proven themselves financially.

But his position on hormone implants wasn't popular, and had resulted in some hot exchanges with other cattlemen. Cattle at the Tremayne ranch weren't implanted, and Harden was fervently against the artificial means of beef growth.

"Damn it, it's like using steroids on a human," he argued with the older cattleman. "And we still don't know the long-range effects of consumption of implanted cattle on human beings!"

"You're talking a hell of a financial loss, all the same!" the other argued hotly. "Damn it, man, I'm operating in the red already! Those implants you're against are the only thing keeping me in business. More weight means more money. That's how it is!"

"And what about the countries that won't import American beef because of the implants?" Harden shot back. "What about moral responsibility for what may prove to be a dangerous and unwarranted risk to public health?"

"We're already getting heat for the pesticides we use leaching into the water table," a deep, familiar voice interrupted. "And I won't go into environmentalists claiming grazing is responsible for global warming or the animal rights people who think branding our cattle is cruel, or the government bailing out the dairy industry by dumping their tough, used-up cows on the market with our prime beef!"

That did it. Before Harden could open his mouth, his workshop was shot to hell. He gave up trying to call for order and sat down to drink his coffee.

Evan sat back down beside him, grinning. "Saved your beans, didn't I, pard?" he asked.

Harden gestured toward the crowd. "What about theirs?" he asked, indicating two cattlemen who were shoving each other and red in the face.

"Their problem, not mine. I just didn't want to have to save you from a lynch mob. Couldn't you be a little less opinionated?"

Harden shrugged. "Not my way."

"So I noticed." Evan stood up. "Well, we might as well go and eat lunch. When we come back we can worry about how to dispose of the carnage." He grimaced as a blow was struck nearby.

Harden pursed his lips, his blue eyes narrowing amusedly. "And leave just when things are getting interesting?"

"No." Evan stood in front of him. "Now, look here..."

It didn't work. Harden walked around him and right into a furious big fist. He returned the punch with a hard laugh and waded right into the melee. Evan sighed. He took off his Stetson and his jacket, rolled up the sleeves of his white cotton shirt and loosened his tie. There was such a thing as family unity.

Later, after the police came and spoiled all the fun, Harden and Evan had a quiet lunch in their suite while they patched up the cuts.

"We could have been arrested," Evan muttered between bites of his sandwiches.

"No kidding." Harden swallowed down the last of his coffee and poured another cup from the carafe. He had a bruise on one cheek and another, with a cut, lower on his jaw. Evan had fared almost as badly. Of course, the competition downstairs looked much worse.

"You had a change of clothes," Evan muttered, brushing at blood spots on his white shirt. "I have to fly home like this."

"The stewardesses will be fascinated by you. You'll probably have to turn down dates all the way home."

Evan brightened. "Think so?"

"You look wounded and macho," Harden agreed. "Aren't women supposed to love that?"

"I'm not sure. I lost my perspective when they started carrying guns and bodybuilding. I think the ideal these days is a man who can cook and do housework and likes baby-sitting." He shuddered. "Kids scare me to death!"

"They wouldn't if they were your own."

Evan sighed, and his dark eyes had a faraway look. "I'm too old to start a family."

"My God, you're barely thirty-four!"

"Anyway, I'd have to get married first. Nobody wants me."

"You scare women," Harden replied. "You're the original clown. All smiles and wit. Then something upsets you and you lose your temper and throw somebody over a fence."

Evan's dark eyes narrowed, the real man showing through the facade as he remembered what had prompted that incident. "That yellow-bellied so-and-so put a quirt to my new filly and beat her bloody.

He's damned lucky I didn't catch him until he got off the property in his truck.''

"Any of us would have felt that way," Harden agreed. "But you're not exactly what you seem to be. I may scare people, but I'm always the same. You're not."

Evan dropped his gaze to his coffee, the smile gone. "I got used to fighting when I was a kid. I had to take care of the rest of you, always picking on guys twice your size."

"I know." Harden smiled involuntarily at the memories. "Don't think we didn't appreciate it, either."

Evan looked up. "But once I put a man in the hospital, remember? Never realized I'd hit him that hard. I haven't liked to fight since."

"That was an accident," Harden reminded him. "He fell the wrong way and hit his head. It could have happened to anyone."

"I guess. But my size encourages people to try me. Funny thing, it seems to intimidate women." He shrugged. "I guess I'll be a bachelor for life."

Harden opened his mouth to correct that impression, but the phone rang and claimed his attention. He picked it up and answered, listening with an amused face.

"Sure. I'll be down in ten minutes."

He hung up. "Imagine that. They want me to do another hour. My audience has been bragging that this was the best workshop they'd ever attended. Not boring, you see."

Evan burst out laughing. "Well, you owe that to me."

Harden glared at him. "You can only come back if you promise to keep your mouth shut."

"Bull. You enjoyed it." He stretched hugely. "Anyway, it got your mind off the woman, didn't it?"

Harden was actually lost for words. He just stared at the bigger man.

"It's the timing, isn't it?" Evan asked seriously. "She's newly widowed and you think she's too susceptible. But if she was in that kind of condition, she sure as hell needs someone."

"It's still the wrong time," he replied quietly.

Evan shrugged. "No harm in keeping the door open until it is the right time, is there?" he asked with a grin.

Harden thought about what Evan had said for the rest of the afternoon, even after the other man had caught his flight back to Jacobsville. No, there wouldn't really be any harm in keeping his door open. But was it what he wanted? A woman like Miranda wasn't fit for ranch life, even if he went crazy and got serious about her. She was a city girl from Chicago with a terrible tragedy to put behind her. He was a loner who hated city life and was carrying around his own scars. It would never work.

But his noble thoughts didn't spare his body the anguish of remembering how it had been with Miranda that morning, how fiercely his ardor had affected both of them. All that silky softness against him, her warm, sweet mouth begging for his, her arms holding fast. He groaned aloud as he pictured that slender body naked on white sheets. As explosive as the passion between them was, a night with her would surpass his wildest dreams of ecstasy, he knew it would.

It was the thought of afterward that disturbed him. He might not be able to let her go. That was what stopped him when he placed his hand hesitantly over the telephone and thought about finding her number in the directory and calling her. Once he'd known her intimately, would he be capable of walking away? He stared at the telephone for a long time before he turned away from it and went to bed. No, he told himself. He'd been right in the first place. The timing was all wrong, not only for Miranda, but for himself. He wasn't ready for any kind of commitment.

Miranda was thinking the same thing, back at her own apartment house. But she had the number of the Carlton Arms under her nervous fingers. She stared at it while she sat on her sofa in the lonely apartment, and she wanted so badly to phone, to ask for Harden Tremayne, to...

To what? she asked herself. She knew she'd already been enough trouble to him. But she'd just finished giving her baby furniture to a charity group, and she was sick and depressed. Even though she wasn't in love with Tim anymore, she grieved for the child she was carrying. It would have been so wonderful to have a baby of her own to love and care for.

None of which was Harden's problem. He'd been reluctantly kind, as he would have been to anybody in trouble. He'd said as much. But she was remembering the way they'd kissed each other, and the heat of passion that she'd never felt with anyone else. It made her so hungry. She'd expected love and forever from marriage. She'd had neither. Even sex, so mysterious and complicated, hadn't been the wonderful experience she'd expected. It had been painful at first, and then just unpleasant. Bells didn't ring and the earth didn't move. In fact, she was only just able to admit to herself that she'd never felt any kind of physical attraction to Tim. She'd briefly imagined herself in love with him, but he'd been a stranger when they married. As she lived with him, she began to see the real man under the brash outgoing reporter, and it was a person she didn't like very much. He was selfish and demanding and totally insensitive.

Harden didn't seem to be that kind of man at all. He was caring, even if he was scary and cold on the surface. Underneath, he was a smoldering volcano of emotion and she wanted to dig deeper, to see how consuming a fire they could create together. With him, intimacy would be a wondrous thing. She knew it. Probably he did, too, but he was keeping his distance tonight. Either he wasn't interested or he thought it was too soon after her loss.

He was right. It was too soon. She crumpled the piece of paper where she'd written the number of the hotel. She was still grieving and much too vulnerable for a quick love affair, which was probably all he'd be able to offer her. He'd said he was a loner and he didn't seem in any hurry to marry. He'd been all too eager to get away from her, in fact. She put the paper in the trash can. It was just as well. She'd managed to get through work today without breaking down, and she'd manage the rest of her life the same way. It wasn't really fair to involve another person in the mess her mind was in.

She put on her nightgown and climbed under the covers. Finally she slept.

Chapter Four

Harden slept badly. When he woke, he only retained images of the torrid dreams that had made him so restless. But a vivid picture of Miranda danced in front of his eyes.

He was due to go home today. The thought, so pleasantly entertained two days before, was unpalatable today. Texas was a long way from Illinois. He probably wouldn't see Miranda again.

He dragged himself out of bed, hitching up the navy-blue pajama trousers that hung low on his narrow hips. He rubbed a careless hand over his broad, hair-matted chest and stared out the window, scowling. Ridiculous, what he was thinking. There were responsibilities at home, and he'd already told himself how impossible it was to entertain ideas about her.

Impossible. He repeated the word even as he turned and picked up the telephone directory. He didn't know Miranda's maiden name, which made phoning her brother to ask where she worked out of the question. His only chance was to call her apartment and catch her before she left.

He found Tim Warren's name in the new directory and dialed the number before he could change his mind.

It rang once. Twice. Three times. He glanced at his watch on the bedside table. Eight o'clock. Perhaps she'd left for work. It rang four times. Then five. With a long sigh, he started to hang it up. Maybe it was fate, he thought with disappointment.

Then, just as the receiver started down, her soft voice said, "Hello?"

His hand reversed in midair. "Miranda?" he asked softly.

Her breath caught audibly. "Harden!" she cried as if she couldn't believe her ears.

His chest expanded with involuntary pleasure, because she'd recognized his voice instantly. "Yes," he replied. "How are you?"

She sat down, overcome with excited pleasure. "I'm better. Much better, thank you. How are you?"

"Bruised," he murmured dryly. "My brother helped me into a free-for-all at the workshop yesterday."

"Somebody insulted Texas," she guessed.

"Not at all," he replied. "We were discussing hormone implants and the ecology at the time."

"Really?"

He laughed in spite of himself. "I'll tell you all about it over lunch."

She caught her breath. It was more than she'd dared hope for. "You want to take me to lunch?" she asked breathlessly.

"Yes."

"Oh, I'd like that," she said softly.

He didn't want to have to admit how much he'd like it himself. He put on his watch. "When should I pick you up? And where?"

"At eleven-thirty," she said. "I go early so that we won't be all out of the office at the same time. It's in the Brant building. Three blocks north of your hotel." She gave him directions and the office number. "Can you find it?"

"I'll find it."

He hung up before she had time to reply. This was stupid, he told himself. But all the same, he had a delicious feeling of anticipation. He phoned the ranch to tell them he wouldn't be home for another day or two.

His mother, Theodora, answered the phone. "Harden?" she asked. "The car won't start."

"Did you put it in park before you tried to start it?" he asked irritably.

There was a long pause. "Just because I did that once . . . !" she began defensively.

"Six times."

"Whatever. Well, no, actually, I guess it's in drive."

"Put it in Park and it will start. Is Donald back?"

"No, he won't be home until next week."

"Then tell Evan he'll have to manage. I'm going to be delayed for a few days."

There was another pause. "Evan's got a split lip."

"I've got a black eye. So what? You have to expect a little spirit when you get a roomful of cattlemen."

"I do wish you wouldn't encourage him to get into fights."

"For God's sake, Theodora, he started it!" he raged.

"Can't you ever call me Mother?" she asked in an unconsciously wistful tone.

"Will you give the message to Evan?" he replied stiffly.

She sighed. "Yes, I'll tell him. You wouldn't like to explain what's going on up there, I suppose?"

"There's nothing to tell."

"I see. I don't know why I keep hoping for the impossible from you, Harden," she said dully. "When I know full well that you'll never forgive me."

Her voice was sad. He felt guilty when he heard that note in her voice. Theodora was flighty, but she had a big heart and a sensitive spirit. Probably he hurt her every time he talked to her.

"Evan can reach me here at the hotel if he needs me," he said, refusing to give in to the impulse to talk—to really talk—to her.

"All right. Goodbye, Son."

She hung up and he stared at the receiver, the dial tone loud in his ears. He'd never asked her about his father, or why she hadn't thought of an abortion when she knew she was carrying him. Certainly it would have made her life easier. He wondered why that thought occurred to him now. He put down the receiver and got dressed.

At eleven-thirty sharp, he walked into the law office where Miranda worked. He was wearing a tan suit, a subdued striped tie, a pearly Stetson and hand-tooled leather boots. He immediately drew the eyes of every woman in the office, and Miranda got up from her desk self-consciously. She couldn't tear her eyes away from him, either.

In her neat red-patterned rayon skirt and white blouse with a trendy scarf draped over one shoulder she looked pretty, too. Harden glared at her because she pleased his senses. This whole thing was against his will. He should be on his way home, not hanging around here with a recently widowed woman.

Miranda felt threatened by the dark scowl on his face. He looked as if he'd rather be anywhere but here, and she felt a little self-conscious herself at what amounted to a date only weeks after she was widowed. But it was only lunch, after all.

"I'll just get my purse," she murmured nervously.

"I could go with you and carry it," Janet, her co-worker, volunteered in a stage whisper. She grinned at Harden, but he had eyes for no one except Miranda. He gave the other employee a look that could have frozen fire.

"Thanks, anyway," Miranda murmured when Janet began to appear threatened. She grabbed her purse, smiled halfheartedly at the other woman, and rushed out the door.

"Does your friend always come on to men like that?" he asked as he closed the door behind her.

"Only when they look like you do," she said shyly.

He cocked an eyebrow and pulled his hat lower over his eyes. "I don't take one woman out and flirt with another one."

"I'm absolutely sure that Janet won't forget that," she assured him.

He took her arm as they got into the elevator. "What do you feel like? Hamburgers, fish, barbecue, or Chinese?"

"I like Chinese," she said at once.

"So do I." He pushed the Down button and stared at her from his lounging posture against the wall as it began to move. Her hair was done in some complicated plait down her back, but it suited her. So did the dangly silver earrings she was wearing. His eyes slid down to the dainty strappy high heels on her pretty feet and back up again.

"Will I do?" she asked uncertainly.

"Oh, you'll do," he agreed quietly. His eyes narrowed with faint anger while he searched hers. "I'm supposed to be on a one o'clock flight home."

She swallowed. "Are you?" she asked, and her face fell.

He noticed her disappointment. It had to mean that she was as fascinated by him as he was by her, but it didn't do much for his conscience. This was all wrong.

"Do you have time to take me to lunch?" she asked worriedly.

"I canceled the flight," he said then. He didn't add that he hadn't yet decided when he was going home. He didn't want to admit how drawn he was to her.

Her silver eyes went molten as they met his and she couldn't hide her pleasure.

That made it worse, somehow. "It's insane!" he said roughly. "Wrong time, wrong place."

"Then why aren't you leaving town?" she asked.

"Why didn't you say no when I asked you out to lunch?" he shot right back.

She felt, and looked, uncertain. "I couldn't," she replied hesitantly. "I . . . wanted to be with you."

He nodded. "That's why I'm here," he said.

The elevator stopped while they were staring at each other. His pale blue eyes glittered, but he didn't make a move toward her, even though it was killing him to keep the distance between them.

The doors opened and he escorted her out the front door, his fingers hard on her upper arm, feeling the thinness through the blouse.

"You've lost weight, haven't you?" he asked as they walked down the crowded street toward the Chinese restaurant he'd seen on the way to her building.

"A little. I've always been thin."

A small group of people came rushing past them and knocked against Miranda. Even as she lost her footing, Harden's arm was around her, pressing her against him.

"Okay?" he asked softly, his eyes watchful, concerned.

She couldn't look away from him. He hypnotized her. "Yes. I'm fine, thanks."

His fingers contracted on her waist. She was wrapping silken bonds around him. He didn't know if he liked it, but he couldn't quite resist her.

Her heart hammered crazily. He looked odd; totally out of humor, but fascinated at the same time.

In fact, he was. His own helplessness irritated him.

Neither of them moved, and he almost groaned out loud as he forced himself to turn and walk on down the street.

Miranda felt the strength in his powerful body and felt guilty for noticing it, for reacting to it. She walked beside him quietly, her thoughts tormenting her.

The restaurant wasn't crowded. Miranda settled on the day's special, while Harden indulged his passion for sweet-and-sour pork. When he reached for the hot mustard sauce for his egg roll, she shuddered.

"You aren't really going to do that, are you?" she asked. "You might vanish in a puff of smoke. Haven't you ever heard of spontaneous combustion?"

"I like Tabasco sauce on my chili," he informed her, heaping the sauce on the egg roll. "I haven't had taste buds since 1975."

"I still can't watch."

He smiled. "Suit yourself."

He ate the egg roll with evident enjoyment while she sipped more hot tea. When he finished she stared at him openly.

"I'm waiting for you to explode," she explained when his eyebrows lifted in a question. "I think that stuff is really rocket fuel."

He chuckled. It had been a long time since he'd felt like laughing. It surprised him that Miranda was the catalyst, with all the grief she'd suffered so recently. He searched her eyes curiously as a new thought occurred to him.

"You forget when you're with me, don't you?" he asked. "That's why you came back to the hotel night before last instead of insisting that I take you home."

She stared at him. Finally she nodded. "I stop brooding when I'm around you. I don't understand why, really," she added with a quiet sigh. "But you make it all go away."

He didn't reply. He stared down at his cup with eyes that hardly saw it. She attracted him. He'd thought it was mutual. But apparently he was only a balm for her grief, and that disturbed him. He should have followed his instincts and gone home this morning.

"Did I even say thank you?" she asked.

"You said it." He finished his tea and studied her over the rim of the small cup. "When do you have to be back?"

She glanced at the big face of his watch. "At one-thirty." She hesitated. "I guess you think I'm only using you, to put what happened out of my mind," she said suddenly. "But I'm not. I enjoy being with you. I don't feel so alone anymore."

She might have read his mind. The tension in him relaxed a little. He finished his tea. "In that case, we'll go the park and feed the pigeons."

Her face lit up. That would mean a few more precious minutes in his company. It also meant that he wasn't angry with her.

"No need to ask if you'd like to," he murmured dryly. "Finish your tea, little one."

She drained the cup obediently and got up, waiting for him to join her.

They strolled through the park overlooking the lake. The wind was blowing, as it always did, and she enjoyed the feel of it in her hair. He bought popcorn from a vendor and they sat on a bench facing the water, tossing the treat to the fat pigeons.

"We're probably giving them high-blood pressure, high cholesterol, and heart trouble," she observed as the birds waddled from one piece of popcorn to the next.

He leaned back on the bench, one arm over the back, and looked down at her indulgently. "Popcorn is healthier than bread. But you could ask them to stop eating it."

She laughed. "I'd be committed."

"Oh, I'd save you." He tossed another kernel to the pigeons and stared out at the lake, where sailboats were visible in the distance. "Jacobsville doesn't have a lake this size," he murmured. "We have a small one on the ranch, but we're pretty landlocked back home."

"I've gotten used to seeing the sailboats and motorboats here," she sighed, following his gaze. "I can see them out the office window on a clear day." She tucked loose strands of hair back behind her ear. "The wind never stops. I suppose the lake adds to it."

"More than likely," he replied. "I used to spend a good bit of time down in the Caribbean. It blows nonstop on the beach as well."

"And out on the plains," she murmured, smiling as she remembered her childhood on a ranch in South Dakota. Something she hadn't told him about.

"Pretty country," he said. "We had an interest in a ranch up in Montana, a few years back. It folded. Bad water. Salt leaching killed the land."

"What kind of cattle do you raise?" she asked.

"Purebred Santa Gertrudis mostly. But we run a cow-calf operation alongside it. That means we produce beef cattle," he explained.

She knew that instantly, and more. She'd grown up in ranching country and knew quite a bit about how beef was produced, but she didn't say so. It was nicer to let him explain how it worked, to sit and listen to his deep, quiet voice.

Her lunch hour was up before she realized it. She got to her feet with real reluctance. "I have to go," she said miserably.

He stood up beside her, his pale blue eyes on her downbent head. He rammed his hands into his pockets and glowered at the dejected picture she made. He knew what he had to do, though.

"I'm going home, Miranda," he said shortly.

She wasn't surprised. He'd acted as if he was here against his better judgment, and she couldn't blame him. Her conscience was beating her over the head, because it didn't feel right to be going on a date when her husband was only dead a month.

She looked up. His expression gave nothing away, but something was flickering in his eyes. "I don't know what would have happened to me if it hadn't been for you," she said. "I won't forget you."

His jaw went taut. He wouldn't forget her, either, but he couldn't put it into words.

He turned, beginning the long walk back to her office. It shouldn't have felt so painful. In recent years, there hadn't been a woman he couldn't take in his stride and walk away from. But Miranda looked lost and vulnerable.

"I'm a loner," he said irritably. "I like it that way. I don't need anyone."

"I suppose I'm not very good at being alone," she replied. "But I'll learn. I'll have to."

"You were alone before you married, weren't you?" he asked.

"Not really. I lived with Sam and Joan. Then I decided that enough was enough, so I improved myself and found Tim." She sighed wearily. "But I guess I was alone, if you stop and think about it. Even after Tim and I got married, he always had someplace to go without me. Then I got pregnant, but that wasn't meant to be." She felt her body tauten. It was still hard to think about the child she'd lost; about her part in its loss. She felt a minute's panic at losing Harden, now that she'd begun to depend on him. She glanced at him. "I married too quickly and I learned a hard lesson: there are worse things than your own company."

"Yes." He let his pale eyes slide down to meet hers. "You've given me a new perspective on women. I suppose there are some decent ones in the world."

She smiled sadly. "High praise, coming from you."

"Higher than you realize. I meant it. I hate women," he said curtly.

That was sad. She knew it was probably because of his mother, and she wondered if he'd ever tried to understand how his mother had felt. If he'd never loved, how could he?

"You've been very kind to me."

"I'm not a kind man, as a rule. You bring out a side of me I haven't seen before."

She smiled. "I'm glad."

"I'm not sure I am," he said. "Will you be all right?"

"Yes. I've got Sam and Joan, you know. And the worst of it is over now. I'll grieve longer for the baby than I will for Tim, I'm afraid."

"You're young. There can be other babies."

Her eyes turned wistful. "Can there? I'm not so sure."

"You'll marry again. Don't give up on life because you had some hard knocks. We all have them. But we survive."

"I never found out what yours were," she reminded him.

He shrugged. "It does no good to talk about them." He stopped in front of her office building. "Take care of yourself, Miranda."

She looked up at him with quiet regret. He was a very special man, and she was a better person for having known him at all. She wondered how different her life would have been if she'd met him before Tim. He was everything Tim hadn't been. He was the kind of man a woman would do anything for. But he was out of her reach already. It made her sad.

"I will. You, too." She sighed. "Goodbye, Harden."

He searched her eyes for a long minute, until her body began to throb. "Goodbye."

He turned and walked away. She watched him helplessly, feeling more lost and alone than ever before.

Harden was feeling something similar. It should have been easy to end something that had never really begun, but it wasn't. She'd looked so vulnerable when he'd left her. Her face haunted him already, and he was only a few yards away.

If only his mind would stop remembering the softness of Miranda's silver eyes, looking up at him so trustingly. He'd never had a woman lean on him before. He was surprised to find that he liked it. He felt himself hesitating.

His steps slowed. He muttered a harsh curse as he turned. Sure enough, Miranda was still standing there, looking lost. He felt himself walking back to her without understanding how it happened. A minute later, he was towering over her, seeing his own helpless relief mirrored in her soft gray eyes.

Her eyes searched his in the silence that followed.

"What time do you get off—five?" he asked tersely.

She could hardly get the word out. "Yes."

He nodded. "I'll pick you up."

"The traffic is terrible..."

He glared at her. "So what?"

She reached out and touched his arm. "You came back."

"Don't think I wanted to," he told her flatly. "But I can't seem to help myself. Go to work. We'll find some exotic place for supper."

"I can cook," she volunteered. "You could come to my apartment."

"And let you spend half the night in the kitchen after you've worked all day?" he asked. He shook his head. "No way."

"Are you sure?"

He smiled faintly. "No. But we'll manage. I'll be out front when you get off. Are you usually on time?"

"Always," she said. "The boss is a stickler for promptness, even when it comes to getting off from work." She stared up at him for a long moment, ignoring passers-by, her heart singing. "Oh, I'm glad you stayed!" she said softly.

"Even if it was against my better instincts?"

"Will it help if I tell you that you might have saved my sanity, if not my life?" she replied.

He studied her for a long moment. "It will help. I'll see you later."

He watched her go inside the building, his face still taut with reluctant need. It surprised him that he could feel at all, when his emotions had lived in limbo for so long.

After he left her, he spent the rest of the day getting acquainted with the city. It was big and busy and much like any other city, but he enjoyed the huge modern sculptures and the ethnic restaurants and the museums. He felt like any tourist by the time he'd showered and changed and gone back to pick up Miranda.

She was breathless when she got to him in the lobby.

"I ran all the way," she panted, holding on to the sleeves of his gray suit coat as she fought for breath. "We were late today, of all days!"

He smiled faintly. "I would have waited."

"I guess I knew that, but I hurried, all the same."

He escorted her to the car and put her inside. "I found a Polynesian place. Ever had poi?"

"Not yet. That sounds adventurous. But I really would like to change first . . ."

"No problem." He remembered without being told where her apartment was. He drove her there, finding a parking spot near the house—a miracle in itself, she told him brightly.

He waited in the living room while she changed. His curiosity got the best of him and he browsed through her bookshelf and stared around, learning about her. She liked biographies, especially those that dealt with the late nineteenth century out West. She had craft books and plenty of specific works on various Plains Indian tribes. There were music books, too, and he looked around instinctively for an instrument, but he didn't find one.

She came out, still hurriedly fastening a pearl necklace over the simple black sheath dress she was wearing with strappy high heels. Her hair was loose, but neatly brushed, hanging over her shoulders like black silk.

"Is this all right?" she asked. "I haven't been out much. Tim liked casual places. If I'm overdressed, I can change, but you're wearing a suit and I thought—!"

He moved close to her during the rush of words and quietly laid his thumb square over her pretty lips, halting them.

"You look fine," he said. "There's no reason to be nervous."

"Isn't there?" she asked, forcing a smile. "I'm all thumbs. I feel as if I'm eighteen again." The smile faded. "I shouldn't be doing this. My husband has only been dead a few weeks, and I lost my baby. I shouldn't go out, I should still be in mourning," she stammered, trying to make sense of what was happening to her.

"We both know that," he agreed. "It doesn't help very much."

"No," she replied with a sad smile.

He sighed heavily. "I can go back to my hotel and pack," he said, "or we can go out to dinner, which is the best solution. If it helps, think of us as two lonely people helping each other through a bad time."

"Are you lonely, Harden?" she asked.

He drew in a slow breath and his hand touched her hair very lightly. "Yes, I'm lonely," he said harshly. "I've never been any other way."

"Always on the outside looking in," she murmured, watching his face tauten. "Yes, I know how it feels, because in spite of Sam and Joan, that's how it was with me. I thought Tim would make it all come right, but he only made things worse. He wanted what I couldn't give him."

"This?" he asked, and slowly, slowly, traced around the firm, full curve of her mouth, watching her lips part and follow his finger helplessly. She reacted to him instantly. It made his head spin with delicious sensations.

She caught his wrist, staying his hand. "Please," she whispered, swallowing hard. "Don't."

"Does it make you feel guilty to let me pleasure you?" he asked quietly. "It isn't something I offer very often. I meant what I said, I detest women, as a rule."

"I guess I do feel guilty," she admitted. "I was driving and two lives were lost." Her voice broke. "It was *my* fault...!"

He drew her to him and enveloped her in his hard arms, holding her while the tears fell. "Give yourself time. Desperation won't solve the problem or stop the pain. You have to be kind to yourself."

"I hate myself!"

His lips brushed her temple. "Miranda, everyone has a secret shame, a searing guilt. It's part of being human. Believe me, you can get through the pain if you just think past it. Think ahead. Find something to look forward to, even if it's just a movie or eating at a special restaurant or a holiday. You can survive anything if you have something to look forward to."

"Does it work?"

"It got me through my own rough time," he replied.

She drew back, brushing at her tear-streaked cheeks. "Want to tell me what it was?" she asked with a watery smile.

He smiled back, gently. "No."

She sighed. "You're a very private person, aren't you?"

"I think that's a trait we share." He drew back, pulling her upright with him. The neckline of her dress was high and very demure and he lifted an eyebrow at it.

"I dress like a middle-aged woman, isn't that what you're thinking?" she muttered.

He laughed out loud. "I'm afraid so. Don't you have something a little more modern in your closet?"

She shifted her shoulders. "Yes. But I can't wear low necklines because..."

He tilted her chin up. "Because...?"

She flushed a little and dropped her eyes. "I'm not exactly overendowed. I, well, I cheat a little and if I wear something low cut, you can tell."

He pursed his lips and dropped his eyes to her bodice. "Now you've intrigued me."

She moved a little away from him, feeling shy and naive. "Hadn't we better go?"

He smiled. "Nervous of me, Miranda?"

"I imagine most women are," she said seriously, searching his hard face. "You're intimidating."

"I'll try not to intimidate you too much," he promised, and held the door open for her. As she passed him on the way out, he wondered how long he could contain his desire for her without doing something irrevocable.

Chapter Five

For the next few days, Harden tried not to think about the reasons he shouldn't be with Miranda. She was in his blood, a sweet fever that he couldn't cure. The more he tried to resist her, the more his mind tormented him. Eventually, he gave in to it, because there was nothing else he could do.

Work was piling up back at home because he wasn't there to help Evan. His mind was anywhere except on the job these days. More and more, his waking and sleeping hours were filled with the sight of Miranda's lovely face.

He hated his obsession with her. He was a confirmed bachelor, well able to resist a pretty face. Why couldn't he escape this one? Her figure was really nothing spectacular. She was pretty, but so were plenty of other women. No, it was her nature that drew him;

her sweet, gentle nature that gave more than it asked. She enveloped him like a soft web, and fighting it only entangled him deeper.

During the past few days, they'd been inseparable. They went out to dinner almost every night. He took her dancing, and last night they'd gone bowling. He hadn't done that in years. It felt unfamiliar to be throwing balls down alleys, and when he scored, Miranda was as enthusiastic as if she'd done it herself.

She laughed. She played. He was fascinated by the way she came out of her shell when she was with him, even if he did get frequent and disturbing glimpses of the anguish in her silver eyes.

He didn't touch her. That was one luxury he wouldn't allow himself. They were too explosive physically, as he'd found out the morning he'd taken her home from the hotel. Instead, they talked. He learned more about her, and told her more about himself than he'd shared with anyone else. It was a time of discovery, of exploration. It was a time between worlds, and it had to end soon.

"You're brooding again," she remarked as he walked her to her door. They'd been out to eat, again, and he'd been preoccupied all night.

"I've got to go back," he said reluctantly. He looked down at her with a dark frown. "I can't stay any longer."

She turned and unlocked her door slowly, without glancing his way. She'd expected it. It shouldn't have surprised her.

"I'm a working man, damn it," he said shortly. "I can't spend my life wandering around Chicago while you're in your office!"

She did look at him then, with soft, sad eyes. "I know, Harden," she said softly.

He shoved his hands into his pockets. "Can you write a letter?"

She hesitated. "A letter? Well, yes...I've never had anybody to write to, of course," she added.

"You can write to me," he said, his voice terse with impatience and irritation. "It isn't the same as having time to spend together, but it's better than phone calls. I can't talk on the phone. I can never think of anything to say."

"Me, too," she said, smiling up at him. Her heart raced. He had to be interested if he was willing to keep in touch. It lifted her spirits.

"Don't expect a letter a day," he cautioned her. "I'm not that good at it."

"I don't have your mailing address," she said.

"Get me a piece of paper. I'll write it down for you."

He followed her into the apartment and waited while she produced a pad and pen. He scribbled the ranch's box number and zip code in a bold, black scrawl and gave it to her.

"This is mine," she said, taking the pad and writing down her own address. She put the pad aside and looked up at him. "You've made life bearable for me. I wish I could do something that nice for you."

His teeth clenched. He let his eyes run down the length of the black strappy dress she was wearing to long legs encased in nylon and sling-back pumps with rhinestone buckles. His gaze came back up to her loosened dark hair and her soft oval face and her trusting silver eyes.

"You could, if you wanted to," he said huskily.

She swallowed. Here it was. She hadn't mistaken his desire for her, and now he was going to ask something that she didn't know if she could give.

"Harden...I...I don't like intimacy," she said nervously.

His eyebrows arched. He hadn't expected her to be so blunt. "I wasn't going to ask you to come to bed with me," he murmured dryly. "Even I have more finesse than that."

She took a steadying breath. "Oh."

"But while we're on the subject," he said, pushing the door shut behind him, "why don't you like intimacy?"

"It's unpleasant," she said flatly.

"Painful?" he probed.

She put her purse on a table and traced patterns on it, without looking at him. Harsh memories flooded into her mind. "Only once," she said hesitantly. "I mean unsatisfying, I guess. Embarrassing and unsatisfying. I never liked it."

He paused behind her, his lean hands catching her waist and turning her, so that she faced him.

"Did he arouse you properly before he took you?" he asked matter-of-factly.

She gasped. Her wide eyes met his as if she couldn't believe what he'd said.

He shrugged. "I don't find it uncomfortable to talk about. Neither should you, at your age."

"I haven't ever talked about it, though," she stammered.

"Your brother is a doctor," he pointed out.

"But, my goodness, Sam is worse than I am," she exclaimed. "He can't even say the word sex in front of people. He's a very repressed man. Straitlaced, isn't that the word? And Joan is a dear, but you can't talk to her about . . . intimacy."

"Then talk to me about it," he replied. "That first morning, when I kissed you, you weren't afraid of being intimate with me, were you?"

She nibbled her lower lip. "No," she said, her face flaming.

"Was it like that with your husband?"

She hesitated. Then she shook her head.

"There's a chemistry between people sometimes," he said, watching her face. "An explosive need that pulls them together. I haven't felt it often, and never quite like this. I gather that you've never felt it at all before."

"That's . . . fairly accurate."

He tucked his hand under her chin and lifted her shy eyes to his. "Sex, in order to be good, has to have that explosive quality. That, and a few other ingredients—like respect, trust, and emotional involvement. It's an elusive combination that most people never find. They settle for what they can get."

"Like I did, you mean," she said.

He nodded. "Like you did." He lifted one lean hand to her face and very lightly traced her mouth, watching it part, watching her breathing change suddenly. "Feel it?" he asked softly. "That tightening in your body when I touch your mouth, the way your breath catches and your pulse races?"

"Yes." She swallowed. "Harden, do you feel it?"

"To the soles of my feet," he replied. He bent and lifted her, very gently, in his arms, his eyes on her face. "Let me make love to you. Set any limits you like."

The temptation made her heart race. She dropped her eyes to his thin mouth and wanted it beyond bearing. "Don't...don't make me pregnant," she whispered. "I don't have anything to use."

His body shuddered. It humbled him that she'd let him go that far. "I don't have anything to use, either, so we can't go all the way together," he said unsteadily. "Does that reassure you?"

"Yes."

He moved toward the bedroom, and stopped when he noticed her eyes darting nervously to the bed.

"He made love to you there," he said suddenly, his eyes blazing as he guessed the reason for her hesitation. He looked down into her face. "Was it always there?"

"Yes," she whispered.

"How about on the sofa?"

Her body tensed with anticipated pleasure. "No."

He whirled on his heel and carried her to the long, cushy sofa. He put her down on it and stood looking at the length of her with eyes that made her body move restlessly.

She felt uneasy. He was probably used to women who were voluptuous and perfectly figured, and she had plenty of inhibitions about her body that Tim had given her. The padded bra had been his idea, because he never thought she was adequate.

Harden saw the hesitation in Miranda's big eyes and wondered at it. He unfastened his tie and tossed it into the chair beside the sofa. His jacket followed. He held her eyes while his hand slowly unbuttoned the white shirt under it, revealing the breadth and strength of his hair-matted chest. He liked the way Miranda's eyes lingered on his torso, the helpless delight in them.

"Do you like what you see?" he asked arrogantly.

"Can't you tell?" she whispered.

He sat down beside her, his hand sliding under her back to find the zipper of her dress. "We'll compare notes."

But her hands caught his arms as she realized what he was going to do. All her insecurities flamed on her face.

He frowned. And then he remembered. His thin mouth pulled into a soft, secretive smile. "Ah, I see. The padded bra," he whispered.

She blushed scarlet, but he only laughed. It wasn't a cruel laugh, either. It was as if he was going to share some delicious secret with her, and wanted her to enjoy it, too.

His hand slowly pulled the zipper down. He ignored the nervous hands trying to stop him. "Will it help if I tell you that size only matters to adolescent boys who never grow up?" he asked softly.

"Tim said . . ."

"I'm not Tim," he whispered as his mouth gently covered hers.

She felt the very texture of his lips as he brushed them lightly over and around hers. He caught her top lip between his teeth and touched it with his tongue, as if he were savoring the taste of the delicate inner flesh. Her breath stopped in her throat because it was very arousing.

And meanwhile, he was sliding the dress off her shoulders, along with her bra straps.

"You . . . mustn't," she protested just once.

He hesitated as the dress slid to the upper curves of her firm breasts. "Why?" he asked softly, his lips touching her mouth as he spoke.

"It's . . . it's too soon," she said, her voice sounding panicky.

"No, that's not the reason," he murmured. He lifted his head and searched her silver eyes. "You think I'll be disappointed when I look at you." He smiled. "You're beautiful, Miranda, and you have a heart as big as all outdoors. The size of your breasts isn't going to matter to me."

The color came into her cheeks again. Even Tim had never said anything so intimate to her.

"So innocent," he said solemnly, all the humor gone. "He didn't leave fingerprints, did he? But I promise you, I will." His hands moved, drawing the fabric away from her firm, high breasts, and he looked down at them with masculine appreciation.

She didn't even breathe. Her heart was racing madly, and she felt her nipples become hard under that silent, intent scrutiny. She might be small, but he wasn't looking at her as if he minded. His eyes were finding every difference in color, in texture, sketching her with the absorption of an artist.

"Sometimes I think God must be an artist," he said, echoing her silent thoughts. "The way He creates perfection with just the right form and mix of colors, the beauty of His compositions. I get breathless looking at a sunset. But I get more breathless looking at you." His eyes finally lifted to hers. "Why are you self-conscious about your size?"

"I..." She cleared her throat. Incredible, to be lying here naked from the waist up and listening to a man talk about her breasts! "Well, Tim said I was too little."

He smiled gently. "Did he?"

He seemed to find that amusing. His hands moved again, and this time she did protest, but he bent and gently brushed her eyelids shut with his mouth as he eased the rest of the fabric down her body. In seconds, he had her totally undressed.

He lifted his head then and looked at her, his eyes soft and quiet as she lay trembling, helpless.

"I won't even touch you," he whispered. "Don't be embarrassed."

"But . . . I've *never*—*!*" she stammered.

"Not even in front of your husband?" he asked.

"He didn't like looking at me," she managed unsteadily.

He sighed softly, his eyes on her breasts, the curve of her waist, her flat belly and the shadow of her womanhood that led to long, elegant legs. "Miranda, I fear for the sanity of any man who wouldn't like looking at you," he said finally. "I swear to God, you knock the breath right out of me!"

Her eyes fell in shocked delight, and landed on a point south of his belt that spoke volumes. She gasped audibly and averted her gaze to his chest.

"I've always tried to hide that reaction with other women," he said frankly. "But I don't mind very much if you see it. I want you very badly. I'm not ashamed of it, even if it is the wrong time. Look at me, Miranda. I don't think you've ever really looked at a man in this condition."

His tone coaxed her eyes back to his body, but she lifted her gaze a little too quickly and he smiled.

"Doesn't it make you uncomfortable?" she blurted out.

"What? Letting you look, or being this way?"

"Both."

He touched her mouth with a lean forefinger. "I'm enjoying every second of it."

"So am I," she whispered as if it were a guilty secret.

"Will you let me touch you?" he asked softly, searching her eyes. "It has to be because you want it. In this, I won't do anything that even hints of force or coercion."

Her head was whirling. She looked at him and fires kindled in her body. She wanted to know what it felt like to have his hands on her, to feel pleasure.

"Will I like it?" she whispered.

He smiled gently. "Oh, I think so," he murmured.

He bent, and very lightly brushed his lips over one firm breast, his teeth grazing the nipple.

She gasped and shivered. "You...didn't tell me you were going to do that!" she exclaimed, her silver eyes like saucers.

He lifted his head and searched them. "Didn't I?" He smiled again. "Is it all right?"

Having him ask her that made her go boneless. Tim had always taken, demanded, hurt her. The funny thing was that she'd thought it would be like pleading if a man asked first, but Harden looked impossibly arrogant and it didn't sound anything like pleading. Her whole body trembled with shocked pleasure.

"Yes," she whispered. "It's all right."

"In that case..."

His lean hands lifted her body in an arch so that his lips could settle and feed on her soft breasts. She couldn't believe what was happening to her. She'd never felt pleasure before. What she'd thought was desire had been nothing more than infatuation, and this was the stark reality. It was hot and sharp-edged and totally overwhelming. She was helpless as she'd never been, living only through the hard mouth that was teaching her body its most sensitive areas, through the hands that were so gently controlling her.

Her hands were in his thick, dark hair and his mouth was suddenly on hers, forcing her lips apart with a tender ferocity that made her totally his.

"Don't panic," he whispered.

She didn't understand until she felt him touch her in a way that even Tim never had. She cried out and arched, her body going rigid.

Harden looked down at her, but he didn't stop, even when he felt her hands fighting him. "Just this, sweetheart," he whispered, watching her eyes. "Just this. Let it happen. It won't hurt."

She couldn't stop. It was like going over a cliff. She responded because it was impossible not to, her face taut with panic, her eyes wild with it. She was enjoying it, and she couldn't even pretend not to. He watched her face, smiling when she began to whimper, feeling her responses, feeling her pleasure. When it spiraled up suddenly and arched her silky body, when she wept and twisted and then cried out, convulsing, he felt as if he'd experienced everything life had to offer.

He cradled her in his arms while she cried, his lips gentle on her closed eyes, sipping away the tears.

"Amazing, what a man can do when he sets his mind to it," he whispered against her mouth. "I'm glad to see that my instincts haven't worn out. Although I've read about that, I've never done it before."

Her eyes flew open. She was still trembling, but through the afterglow of satisfaction, she could see the muted pleasure in his eyes.

"Never?" she exclaimed.

"Why are you shocked?" he asked. "I'm no playboy. Women are still pretty much a mystery to me. Less so now," he added with a wicked gleam in his eyes.

She blushed and hid her face in his throat. His hair-roughened chest brushed her breasts and she stiffened at the pleasurable sensations that kindled in her. Involuntarily she pressed closer, pushing her hard nipples into the thick hair so that they brushed his skin.

He went taut against her. "No," he whispered.

He sounded threatened, and she liked his sudden vulnerability. He'd seen her helpless. She wanted to see him the same way. She brushed against him, drawing her breasts sensually across his broad chest until she felt him shudder. His big hands caught her arms and tightened, but he didn't try to make her move away.

"Here." He lifted her, so that she sat over his taut body, facing him, and then his hands bruised her hips and pulled her closer, so that the force of his arousal was blatant against her soft belly. He wrapped her up, crushing her breasts into his chest, and sat rocking her hungrily.

"Harden," she whispered.

His jaw clenched. He was losing it. "Touch me, sweetheart."

Her hands smoothed over his chest.

"No," he ground out. "Touch me where I'm a man."

She hesitated. His mouth whispered over her closed eyes. He caught one of her hands and slowly smoothed it down over his flat stomach, his breath catching when he pressed it gently to him.

Her heart ran away with her. She'd never touched Tim like that. The intimate feel of Harden's body made her throb all over. She liked touching him. But when he began to slide the zipper down, she jerked her fingers away and buried her hot face in his throat.

"You're right," he said roughly, fastening it back. "I'm letting it go too far. Much too far."

He eased her away and got up, his tall body shivering a little with residual desire as he fumbled a cigarette out of his pocket and lit it. "Put your things back on, little one," he said huskily.

She stared at him with her black dress in her hands. "You don't want me to," she whispered.

His eyes closed. "My God, no, I don't want you to," he ground out. He turned, his face rigid with unsated passion, his body blatant with it. "I want to bury myself inside you!"

She trembled at the stark need. Her lips parted helplessly. "I . . . I'd let you," she said fervently.

His gaze dropped to her breasts and beyond it, to her flat belly. She'd had a baby there. She'd lost the baby and her husband, and he shouldn't be doing this to her. He shouldn't be taking advantage of her vulnerability.

He closed his eyes again and turned away. "Miranda, you aren't capable of making that kind of decision right now. It's too soon."

Too soon. Too soon. She came back to herself all at once. This was the apartment she'd shared with Tim. She'd been pregnant. She'd lost control of the car and killed her husband and her unborn child. And only minutes before, she'd been begging another man to make love to her.

She dragged the black dress over her head and fumbled the zipper up, her face white with reaction. She bundled up the rest of her things and pushed them down beside the sofa cushion, because she was shaking too hard to put them on. What had she done!

Harden had fastened his shirt and put his tie and jacket in place by the time she dressed.

He looked down at her with quiet, somber eyes in a face as hard as stone. "I won't apologize. It was too sweet for words. But it's too soon for lovemaking."

She couldn't meet his eyes. "But, we did . . ."

"I pleasured you," he replied quietly. "By lovemaking, I mean sex. If I stay around here much longer, you'll give yourself to me."

"You make me sound like a terrible weakling." She laughed mirthlessly.

He knelt just in front of her, his hands beside her hips on the sofa. "Miranda, it isn't a weakness or a sin to want someone. But you've got a tragedy to work through. By staying here, I'm only postponing your need to put it behind you, not to mention clouding your grief with desire. I want you, baby," he said huskily, his eyes fierce as they met hers. "I want you just as desperately as you want me, but you've got to be sure it's not just misplaced grief or a crutch. Sex is serious business to me. I don't sleep around, ever."

She wanted to ask him if he ever had. He seemed very experienced, but he didn't sound as if sex was a minor amusement to him. He might be even more innocent than she was, and that made her feel less embarrassed about what she'd let him do.

She searched his face. "Harden, I might not have acted like it, but it's serious business to me, too. Tim was the only man I ever slept with."

"I know." He caught her hand and held the soft palm to his mouth hungrily. "But he never satisfied you, did he?"

She swallowed. Finally she gave in to that blatant stare. "Not like you did, no." She hesitated.

"You want to ask me something," he guessed from that odd look. "Go ahead. What is it?"

"Would it feel like that if I gave myself to you? If we went all the way?" she asked slowly.

His fingers clenched on hers. "I think it might be even more intense," he said gruffly. "Watching you almost sent me over the edge myself."

She reached out and touched his face, adoring the strength of it under her cool fingers. "You...had nothing," she exclaimed belatedly.

He only smiled. "Don't you believe it," he said with a deep, somber look in his pale blue eyes. "And now, I've got to go. I've put it off as long as I can."

He got to his feet. Miranda let him pull her up and her heart was in her eyes as she gazed up at him.

"I'll miss you more than ever, now," she confessed.

He sighed. "I'll miss you, too, little one," he said curtly. "Write to me. I'm as close as the telephone, if you just want to talk. You'll get through this, Miranda. All you need is a little time."

"I know. You made it so much easier, though."

He brushed his fingers through her unruly hair and tilted her face up to his hungry eyes. "It isn't goodbye. Just so long, for a while."

She nodded. "Okay. So long, then."

He bent and kissed her, so tenderly that she almost cried. "Be good."

"I can't be anything else. You won't be here. Harden," she said as he opened the door.

He looked back, his eyebrow arching in a question.

"Just remember," she said with forced humor. "You saved my life. Now you're responsible for it."

He smiled gently. "I won't forget."

He didn't say goodbye. He gave her one long, last look and went out the door, closing it gently behind him. He hadn't really saved her life, she knew, because she hadn't meant to jump off the bridge. But it made her feel good to think that she owed it to him, that he cared enough to worry about her.

She had his address, and she'd write. Maybe when she was through the natural grieving process, he'd come back, and she'd have a second chance at happiness. She closed her eyes, savoring the intimacy she'd shared with him. She wondered how she was going to live until she saw him again.

Chapter Six

Harden was grumpy when he got home. Not that anybody noticed, because he was *always* grumpy. His irritation didn't improve, either, when his brother Connal showed up.

"Oh, God, no, here he comes again!" Evan groaned when the car pulled up just as he and Harden were coming down the steps.

"That's no way to talk about your brother," Harden chided.

"Just wait," the bigger man said curtly.

"I can't stand it!" Connal greeted them, throwing up his hands. "We get all the way to the hospital, I make all the necessary phone calls, and they say it's false labor! Her water hasn't even broken!"

Evan and Harden exchanged glances.

"He needs help," Evan said. "Broken water?"

"You wouldn't understand," Connal said heavily, his lean, dark face worn and haggard. "I've just left her sleeping long enough to ask Mother to come back with me. Pepi needs a woman around right now."

"We'll starve," Evan said miserably.

"No, you won't," Harden muttered. "We have a cook, remember."

"Mother tells Jeanie May what to cook. You'd better worry, too," Evan said shortly. "Even if you don't live here, you're always around when the food goes on the table."

"Don't you two start, I've got enough problems," Connal muttered darkly.

Evan's eyebrows arched. "Don't look at me. You're the one who made Pepi pregnant.

"I wanted children. So did she."

"Then stop muttering and go home."

Connal glared at the bigger man. "Your day will come," he assured Evan. "You'll be walking the streets dreading your own Waterloo in the delivery room, wait and see!"

Evan's face clouded. His usual carefree expression went into eclipse. "Will I?" he asked on a hard laugh. "Don't bet on it."

Connal started to question that look, but Harden stepped in.

"Theodora's in the study looking up something about how to repair bathrooms," he said.

"The plumber will love that," Connal said knowingly. "Don't worry, I'll have her out of here before she bursts another pipe."

"Last one flooded the back hall," Evan recalled. "I opened the door and almost got swept down to the south forty."

"She's got no business trying to fix things. My God, she had a flat tire on the wheelbarrow!" Harden exclaimed.

"Takes talent," Evan agreed. "But don't keep her too long, will you? She takes my side against him," he jerked a thumb at Harden.

"That's nothing new," Harden said, lighting a cigarette. "She knows how I feel about her."

"One day you'll regret that," Connal said. It wasn't something he usually mentioned, but Harden's attitude was getting to him. Part of the reason he'd come for Theodora was that he'd noticed her increasing depression since Harden had come home from his unexplained stay in Chicago.

"Tell Pepi we asked about her," Harden said easily, refusing to rise to the bait.

"I'll do that."

Connal asked about Donald, who was away again with his wife, and after a minute he said goodbye and went into the house, leaving Harden and Evan to go about their business.

Harden climbed behind the wheel before his brother could protest.

"I'm not riding with you," he told Evan flatly. "Your foot's too heavy."

"I like speed," Evan said bluntly.

"Lately, you like it too much." Harden glanced at him and away. "You haven't been yourself since that girl you were dating broke up with you."

Evan's face set and he glanced out the window without speaking.

"I'm sorry," he told Evan. "I'm sorry as hell. But there has to be a woman for you somewhere."

"I'm thirty-four," Evan said quietly. "It's too late. You used to talk about being a minister. Maybe I should consider it myself."

"A minister isn't necessarily celibate," his brother replied. "You're thinking of a priest. You aren't Catholic," he added.

"No, I'm not. I'm the giant in Jack and the Beanstalk," he said wearily. He put his hat back on. "I'm sorry I don't smoke," he murmured, eyeing Harden's smoke. "It might keep me as cool as it seems to keep you."

"I'm not cool." Harden stared out the windshield. "I've got problems of my own."

"Miranda?" Evan asked slowly.

Harden stiffened. His dreams haunted him with the images of Miranda as she'd let him see her that last night at her apartment. The taste of her mouth, the exquisite softness of her body made him shiver with pleasure even in memory. He missed her like hell, but he had to be patient.

He glanced at Evan. He sighed, then, letting it all out. Evan was the only human being alive he could talk to. "Yes."

"You came home."

"I had to. She's so damned vulnerable. I could never be sure it was me she wanted and not a way to avoid coping with the grief."

"Do you want her?"

Harden took a draw from the cigarette and turned his head. His eyes were blazing as the memories washed over him. "Like I want to breathe," he said.

"What are you going to do?"

The broad shoulders lifted and fell. "I don't know. I'll write to her, I guess. Maybe I'll fly to Chicago now and again. Until she's completely over her grief, I don't dare push too hard. I don't want half a woman."

"Strange," Evan said quietly, "thinking about you with a woman."

"It happens to us all sooner or later, didn't Connal say?"

Evan smiled. "Well, Miranda's a dish. When you finally decide to get involved, you sure pick a winner."

"It's more than the way she looks," came the reply. "She's ... different."

"*The* woman usually is," Evan said, his dark eyes sad in his broad face. "Or so they say."

"You'll find out yourself one day, old son."

"Think so? I can hope, I suppose."

"What we both need is a diversion."

Evan brightened. "Great. Let's go to town and wreck a bar."

"Just because you hate alcohol is no reason to do a Carrie Nation on some defenseless bar," his brother told him firmly.

Evan shrugged. "Okay, I'm easy. Let's go to town and wreck a coffee shop."

Harden chuckled softly. "Not until my eye heals completely," he said, touching the yellowish bruise over his cheekbone.

"Spoilsport. Well, I guess we can go to the hardware store and order that butane we need to heat the branding irons."

"That's better."

Harden got his first letter from Miranda the very next day. It didn't smell of perfume, and it was in a perfectly respectable white envelope instead of a colorful one, but it was newsy and warm.

She mentioned that she'd had dinner with her brother and sister-in-law twice, and that she'd started going to their church—a Baptist church—with them on Sunday. He smiled, wondering if he'd influenced her. She wasn't a Baptist, but he was; a deacon in his local church, where he also sang in the choir. She missed seeing him, her letter concluded, and she hoped that he could make time to write her once in a while.

She was going to be shocked, he decided as he pulled up the chair to his desk and started the word processing program on his computer. He wrote several pages, about the new bulls they'd bought and the hopes he had for the crossbreeding program he'd spoken about at the conference in Chicago. When he finished, he chuckled at his own unfamiliar verbosity. Of course, reading over what he'd written, he discovered that it was a totally impersonal letter. There was nothing warm about it.

He frowned, fingering the paper after he'd printed it out. Well, he couldn't very well say that he missed her like hell and wished he was still in Chicago. That would be overdoing it. With a shrug, he signed the letter with a flourish and sealed it before he could change his mind. Personal touches weren't his style. She'd just have to get used to that.

Miranda was so thrilled when she opened the letter two days later that she didn't at first notice the impersonal style of it. It was only after the excitement subsided that she realized he might have been writing it to a stranger.

Consequently she began to wonder if he was really interested in her, or if he was trying to find a way of letting her down, now that they were so far apart. She remembered how sweet it had been in his arms, but that had only been desire on his part. She knew men could fool themselves into thinking they cared about a woman when it was only their glands getting involved. She'd given Harden plenty of license with her body, and it still made her uneasy that she'd been that intimate with him so soon after Tim and the baby. Her own glands were giving her fits, because she couldn't stop remembering how much pleasure Harden had given her. She missed him until it was like being cut in half. But this letter he'd written to her didn't sound like he was missing her. Not at all.

She sat down that night as she watched television and tried to write the same sort of note back. If he wanted to play it cool, she'd do her best to follow his lead. She couldn't let him know how badly she wanted to be with him, or make him feel guilty for the physical closeness they'd shared. She had to keep things light, or she might inadvertently chase him away. She couldn't bear that. If he wanted impersonal letters, then that's what he'd get. She pushed her sadness to the back of her mind and began to write.

From there, it all began to go downhill. Harden frowned over her reply and his own was terse and brief. Maybe she was regretting their time together. Maybe grief had fed her guilt and she wanted him to end it. Maybe what they'd done together was wearing on her conscience and she only wanted to forget. He'd known he was rushing her. Why hadn't he taken more time?

Once he was back at his apartment in Houston, he was putting things into prospective. There was no future with someone like Miranda, after all. She was a city girl. She'd never fit into ranching. He had his eye on a small ranch near Jacobsville and he'd already put a deposit on it. The house wasn't much. He was having it renovated, but even then it wouldn't be a showplace. It was a working ranch, and it would look like one. Miranda would probably hate the hardship of living on the land, even if he did make good money at it.

He stared out his window at the city lights. The office building where the family's corporate offices were located was visible in the distance among the glittering lights of downtown Houston. He sighed wearily, smoking a cigarette. It had been better when he'd kept to himself and brooded over Theodora's indiscretion.

For the first time, he allowed himself to wonder if his mother had felt for his father the way he felt with Miranda. If her heart had fallen victim to a passion it couldn't resist. If she'd loved his father so much that she couldn't refuse him anything, especially a child.

YOU COULD WIN THE
MILLION DOLLAR GRAND PRIZE
IN *Silhouette's* BIGGEST SWEEPSTAKES

THE BIG WIN

6 GAME TICKETS INSIDE!

ENTER TODAY!

IT'S FUN! IT'S FREE!
AND IT COULD MAKE YOU A
MILLIONAIRE

If you've ever played scratch-off lottery tickets, you should be familiar with how our games work. On each of the first four tickets (numbered 1 to 4 in the upper right) there are Pink Metallic Strips to scratch off.

Using a coin, do just that—carefully scratch the PINK strips to reveal how much each ticket could be worth if it is a winning ticket. Tickets could be worth from $10.00 to $1,000,000.00 in lifetime money.

Note, also, that each of your 4 tickets has a unique sweepstakes Lucky Number…and that's 4 chances for a **BIG WIN!**

FREE BOOKS!

At the same time you play your tickets for big prizes, you are invited to play ticket #5 for the chance to get one or more free book(s) from Silhouette. We give away free book(s) to introduce readers to the benefits of the Silhouette Reader Service™.

Accepting the free book(s) places you under no obligation to buy anything! You may keep your free book(s) and return the accompanying statement marked "cancel." But if we don't hear from you, then every month we'll deliver 6 of the newest Silhouette Romance™ novels right to your door. You'll pay just $2.25* each—plus 69¢ delivery per shipment! You may cancel at any time.

Of course, you may play "THE BIG WIN" without requesting any free book(s) by scratching tickets #1 through #4 only. But remember, that first shipment of one or more books is FREE!

PLUS A FREE GIFT!

One more thing, when you accept the free book(s) on ticket #5 you are also entitled to play ticket #6, which is GOOD FOR A GREAT GIFT! Like the book(s), this gift is totally free and yours to keep as thanks for giving our Reader Service a try!

So scratch off the PINK STRIPS on all your BIG WIN tickets and send for everything today! You've got nothing to lose and everything to gain!

*Terms and prices subject to change without notice.   © 1991 HARLEQUIN ENTERPRISES LIMITED
Canadian residents add applicable federal and provincial sales tax.

Here are your BIG WIN Game Tickets, worth from $10.00 to $1,000,000.00 each. Scratch off the PINK METALLIC STRIP on each of your Sweepstakes tickets to see what you could win and mail your entry right away. (SEE OFFICIAL RULES IN BACK OF BOOK FOR DETAILS!)

This could be your lucky day – GOOD LUCK!

TICKET **1**
Scratch PINK METALLIC STRIP to reveal potential value of this ticket if it is a winning ticket. Return all game tickets intact.

LUCKY NUMBER

1Q 101215

TICKET **2**
Scratch PINK METALLIC STRIP to reveal potential value of this ticket if it is a winning ticket. Return all game tickets intact.

LUCKY NUMBER

3A 098058

TICKET **3**
Scratch PINK METALLIC STRIP to reveal potential value of this ticket if it is a winning ticket. Return all game tickets intact.

LUCKY NUMBER

9W 109409

TICKET **4**
Scratch PINK METALLIC STRIP to reveal potential value of this ticket if it is a winning ticket. Return all game tickets intact.

LUCKY NUMBER

5V 100196

TICKET **5**
We're giving away brand new books to selected individuals. Scratch PINK METALLIC STRIP for number of free books you will receive.

FREE BOOKS

AUTHORIZATION CODE

130107-742

TICKET **6**
We have an outstanding added gift for you if you are accepting our free books. Scratch PINK METALLIC STRIP to reveal gift.

FREE GIFT

AUTHORIZATION CODE

130107-742

YES! Enter my Lucky Numbers in THE BIG WIN Sweepstakes and when winners are selected, tell me if I've won any prize. If PINK METALLIC STRIP is scratched off on ticket #5, I will also receive one or more FREE Silhouette Romance™ novels along with the FREE GIFT on ticket #6, as explained on the opposite page.

(C-SIL-R-03/91) 315 CIS ACGZ

NAME _____

ADDRESS _____ APT. _____

CITY _____ PROVINCE _____ POSTAL CODE _____

Offer limited to one per household and not valid to current Silhouette Romance™ subscribers.
© 1991 HARLEQUIN ENTERPRISES LIMITED.

PRINTED IN U.S.A

FOLD AND DETACH ALONG THIS DOTTED LINE—RETURN ALL GAME TICKETS INTACT.

*Carefully
detach card
along dotted
lines and
mail today!
Play
all your
BIG WIN
tickets
and get
everything
you're
entitled to—
including
FREE BOOKS
and a
FREE GIFT!*

**Business
Reply Mail**

No Postage Stamp
Necessary if Mailed
in Canada

Postage will be paid by

SILHOUETTE READER SERVICE
THE BIG WIN SWEEPSTAKES

P.O. Box 609
Fort Erie, Ontario
L2A 9Z9

Canada Post

125

Postes
Canada

He thought about the child Miranda had lost, and wondered how it would be to give her another, to watch her grow big with it. He remembered her soft cries of pleasure, the look of utter completion on her face. His teeth ground together.

He turned away from the window angrily. Miranda wrote him the kind of letter his brothers might, so how could he imagine she cared? She was closing doors between them. She didn't want him. If she did, why hadn't her later letter been as sweet and warm as that first one?

The more he thought about that, the angrier he got. Days turned to weeks, and before he realized it, three months had passed. He was still writing to Miranda, against his better judgment, but their letters were impersonal and brief. He'd all but stopped writing in the past two weeks. Then a client in Chicago asked Evan to fly up and talk to him.

Evan found an excuse not to go. Connal, a brand-new father with a baby boy to play with, was back on the ranch he and Pepi's father owned in West Texas. Donald and Jo Ann were just back from overseas, and Harden's youngest brother said flatly that he wasn't going anywhere for months—he and Jo Ann had had their fill of traveling.

"Looks like you're elected," Evan told Harden with a grin. "Call it fate."

Harden looked hunted. He paced the office. "I need to stay here."

"You need to go," Evan said quietly. "It hasn't gotten better, you know. You look terrible. You've lost weight, and you're working yourself to death. She's had time to get herself back together. Go and see if the magic's still there.''

''She writes me business letters. She's probably dating somebody else by now.''

''Go find out.''

Harden moved irritably. The temptation was irresistible. The thought of seeing Miranda again made him feel warm. He studied the older man. ''I guess I might as well.''

''I'll handle things here. Have a good trip.''

Harden heard those words over and over. He deliberately put off calling Miranda. He met the client, settled his business, and had lunch. He went to a movie. Then, at five, he happened to walk past her office building just about time for her to come out.

He stood by a traffic sign, Western looking in a pale gray suit with black boots and Stetson, a cigarette in his hand. He got curious, interested looks from several attractive women, but he ignored them. He only had eyes for one woman these days, even if he wasn't sure exactly how he felt about her.

A siren distracted him and when he glanced back, Miranda was coming out of the entrance, her dark hair around her shoulders, wearing a pale green striped dress that made his temperature soar. Her long legs were encased in hose, her pretty feet in strappy high heels. She looked young and pretty, even if she was just as thin as she'd been when he left her.

She was fumbling in her purse for something, so she didn't look up until he was standing directly in her path.

Her expression told him everything he wanted to know. It went from shock to disbelief to utter delight in seconds, her huge silvery eyes like saucers as they met his.

"Harden!" she whispered joyously.

"No need to ask if you're glad to see me," he murmured dryly. "Hello, Miranda."

"When did you get here? How long can you stay? Do you have time to get a cup of coffee with me...!"

He touched his forefinger to her soft mouth with a smile, oblivious to onlookers and pedestrians and motorists that sped past them. "I'll answer all those questions later. I'm parked over here. Let's go."

"I was fumbling for change for the bus," she stammered, red-faced and shaken by his unexpected appearance. Her eyes adored him. "I didn't have it. Have you been here long?"

"A few minutes. I got in this morning." He looked down at her. "You're still thin, but you have a bit more color than you did. Is it getting easier?"

"Yes," she said, nodding. "It's amazing what time can accomplish. I think I have things in perspective now. I'm still sad about the baby, but I'm getting over it."

He paused at his rented Lincoln and opened the passenger door for her. "I'm glad."

She waited until he got in beside her and started the car before she spoke. "I didn't know if I'd see you again," she confessed. "Your letters got shorter and shorter."

"So did yours," he said, and his deep voice sounded vaguely accusing.

"I thought maybe my first one made you uncomfortable," she confessed with a smile. "I sort of used yours as a pattern."

He smiled, too, because that explained everything. Now he understood what she'd done, and why.

"I don't know how to write a letter to a woman," he said after a minute, when he'd pulled into traffic and was negotiating lanes. "That was the first time I ever had."

Her face brightened. "I didn't know."

He shrugged. "No reason you should."

"How long can you stay?"

"I had to see a client," he replied. "I did that this morning."

"Then, you're on your way home. I see," she said quietly. She twisted her purse on her lap and stared out at traffic. Disappointment lined her face, but she didn't let him see. "Well, I'm glad you stopped by, anyway. It was a nice surprise."

He cocked an eyebrow. Either she was transparent, or he was learning to read her very well. "Can't wait to get rid of me, can you?" he mused. "I had thought about staying until tomorrow, at least."

Her face turned toward his, and her eyes brightened. "Were you? I could cook supper."

"I might let you, this time," he said. "I don't want to waste the whole evening in a restaurant."

"Do you need to go back to your hotel first?" she asked.

"What for? I'm wearing the only suit I brought with me, and I've got my wallet in my pocket."

She laughed. "Then we can just go straight home."

He remembered where her apartment house was without any difficulty. He parked the car as close to it as he could get, locked it, and escorted her inside.

While she was changing into jeans and a pink knit top, he wandered around her living room. Nothing had changed, except that there were more books. He picked up one of the paperbacks on the table beside the couch and smiled at her taste. Detective stories and romance novels.

"I like Erle Stanley Gardner," he remarked when she was busy in the kitchen.

"So do I," she told him, smiling over her shoulder as she put coffee on to perk. "And I'm crazy about Sherlock Holmes—on the educational channel, you know."

"I watch that myself."

He perched himself on a stool in front of her breakfast bar and folded his arms on it to study her trim figure as she worked. She produced an ashtray for him, but as she put it down, he caught her waist and pulled her between his legs.

"Kiss me," he said quietly, holding her gaze. "It's been a long, dry spell."

"You haven't been kissed in three months?" she stammered, a little nervous of the proximity.

He smiled. "I hate women, remember? Kiss me, before you start on the steak."

She smiled jerkily. "All right." She leaned foreward, closed her eyes, and brushed her mouth softly against his.

His lean hand tangled in her long hair and held her there, taking over, parting her lips, deepening the kiss.

His breath caught at the intensity of it, like a lightning bolt in the silence of the kitchen.

"It isn't enough," he said tersely, drawing back just long enough to crush out his cigarette. Both arms slid around her and brought her intimately close, so that her belly was against his, her face on an unnerving level with his glittery blue eyes. "I've missed you, woman," he whispered roughly.

His mouth met hers with enough force to push her head back against his hand. He was rough because he was starved for her, and it was a mutual thing. She hesitated only for a second before her arms went around his neck and she pressed close with a soft moan, loving the warm strength of his body as she was enveloped against it. She could hear his breath sighing out as his mouth grew harder on hers, bruising her lips, pushing them apart to give him total access to their moist inner softness.

All at once, his tongue pushed past her lips and into her mouth, and a sensation like liquid fire burst in her stomach. It was as intimate as lovemaking. She felt her whole body begin to throb as he tasted her in a quick, hard rhythm. She made a sound she'd never heard from her throat in her life and shuddered as she moved closer to him, her legs trembling against his.

"Yes," he breathed unsteadily into her mouth. "Yes, sweetheart, like...that...!"

He stood up, taking her with him, one lean hand dropping to her hips to grind them into his own. She stiffened at his fierce arousal, but he ignored her instinctive withdrawal.

"It's all right," he whispered. "Relax. Just relax. I won't hurt you."

His voice had the oddest effect on her. The struggle went out of her all at once, and she gave in to him with an unsteady sigh. Her hands pressed gently into his shirt front and lingered there while the kiss went on and on and she felt a slight tremor in his own powerful legs.

He lifted his head finally and looked down at her, breathing unsteadily, fighting to control what he felt for her.

His hands at her waist tightened and the helpless, submissive look on her soft face pushed him over the edge. "Is there anything cooking that won't keep for a few minutes, Miranda?" he asked quietly.

She swallowed. "No. But . . ."

He bent and lifted her gently into his arms and carried her out of the kitchen. "Don't be afraid, little one," he said quietly.

"Harden, I don't . . . I'm still not using anything," she stammered.

He didn't look at her as he walked into her bedroom. "We won't make love."

Her lips parted. They felt sore and they tasted of him when she touched them with her tongue. He laid her down on the bed and stood looking at her for a long moment before he sat down beside her and bent to take her mouth softly under his once again.

The look in his eyes fascinated her. It was desire mingled with irritation and something darker, something far less identifiable. His gaze fell to the unsteady rise and fall of the knit top she was wearing and his hand moved to smooth down her shoulder to her collarbone.

"No bra tonight?" he asked bluntly, meeting her eyes.

She flushed. "I . . ."

He put a long forefinger on her lips. "What we do together is between you and me," he said solemnly. "Not even my own brothers know anything about my personal life. I want very badly to touch you again, Miranda. I think you want it just as much. If you do, there isn't really any reason we can't indulge each other."

She searched his eyes quietly. "I couldn't sleep, for dreaming about how it was between us, last time," she whispered.

"Neither could I," he replied. His hands moved to her waist and brought her into a sitting position. Gently he removed the pink knit top and put it aside, letting his eyes adore her pink and mauve nudity. He smiled when her nipples went hard under the scrutiny.

Her hands touched his lean cheeks hesitantly and she shivered as she drew his face toward her, arching her back to show him what she wanted most.

"Here?" he whispered, obliging her.

She drew in her breath as his mouth opened over her breast, taking almost all of one inside. The faint suction made her tremble, made her nails bite into the shoulders of his suit jacket.

"Too . . . many clothes, Harden," she whispered.

He lifted his head and pressed a soft kiss on her mouth before he stood up. "Yes. Far too many."

He watched her while he removed everything above his belt, enjoying the way her eyes sketched over him.

"Harden," she began shyly, her eyes falling to the wide silver belt.

"No," he said, reading the question in her eyes. He sat down beside her and drew her gently across his lap, moving her breasts into the thick mat of hair over his chest. "If I take anything else off, we'll be lovers."

"Don't you want to?" she asked breathlessly.

"Yes," he said simply. "But it's still too soon for that." He looked down where her pale body was pressed to his darkly tanned one. "I want you to come home with me, Miranda."

Chapter Seven

Miranda didn't believe at first that she'd heard him. She stared at him blankly. "What?"

He met her eyes. "I want you to come home with me," he said, shocking himself as much as he was obviously shocking her. "I want more than this," he added, dragging her breasts sensually against his bare chest. "As sweet as it is, I want to get to know all of you, not just your body."

"But . . . my job," she began.

"I have in mind asking you to marry me, once we've gotten used to each other a little more," he said then, driving the point home. "And don't look so shocked. You know as well as I do that we're going to wind up in bed together. It's inevitable. I'm no more liberated than you are, so we have to do something. Either we get married, or we stop seeing each other altogether. That being the case, you have to come home with me."

"And stay... with you?" she echoed.

"With Theodora. My mother," he clarified it. "I'm buying a place in Jacobsville, but it isn't ready to move into. Even if it was," he added with a rueful smile, "things aren't done that way in Jacobsville. You'd stay with Theodora anyway, to keep everything aboveboard. Or didn't I mention that I was a deacon in our Baptist church?"

"No," she stammered. "You didn't."

"I thought about being a minister once," he murmured, searching her rapt eyes. "But I didn't feel called to it, and that makes the difference. I still feel uncomfortable with so-called modern attitudes. Holding you like this is one thing. Sleeping with you— my conscience isn't going to allow that."

"I was married," she began.

"Yes. But not to me." He smiled gently, looking down to the blatant thrust of her soft breasts with their hard tips brushing against his chest. "And it didn't feel like this, did it?"

"No," she admitted, going breathless when he brushed her body lazily against his. "Oh, no, it didn't feel anything like this!" She pressed even closer, gripping his shoulders tightly. "But you say you hate women. How are you going to manage to marry me?"

"I didn't say I hated you," he replied. His hands tangled in her hair and raised her face to his quiet eyes. "I've never wanted anyone like this," he said simply. "All I've done since I left Chicago is brood over you. I haven't looked at another woman in all that time."

She drew back a little, tingling with pleasure when the action drew his eyes immediately to her breasts. She didn't try to hide them this time.

After a minute, he lifted his eyes to hers and searched them, reading with pinpoint accuracy the pride and pleasure there. "You like it, don't you?" he asked quietly. "You like my eyes on you."

"Yes," she said hesitantly.

"Shame isn't something you should feel with me," he told her. "Not ever. I know too much about you to think you're easy."

She smiled then. "Thank you."

His lean hands smoothed down to her waist, and he shook his head. "I can't imagine being able to do this anytime I please, do you know that?" he said unexpectedly. "I've never had...anyone of my own before." It surprised him to realize that it was true. He'd thought he had, once, but it had been more illusion than reality and he was only discovering it.

"Actually, neither have I," she said. Her eyes ran over his hair-roughened chest down to the ripple of his stomach muscles above his belt and back to the width of his shoulders and his upper arms. "I love to look at you," she said huskily.

"It's mutual." His fingers brushed over the taut curve of one breast, tracing it lovingly. "Don't you *ever* put on a padded bra again," he said shortly, meeting her eyes. "Do you hear me, Miranda?"

She laughed breathlessly. "Yes."

He laughed, too, at his own vehemence. "Too small. My God. Maybe he was shortsighted." He stood up, drawing her with him, his eyes eloquent on her body. "I don't suppose you'd like to cook supper like that..." He sighed heavily.

"Harden!"

"Well, I like looking at you," he said irritably. "Touching you." His fingers brushed over her breasts lovingly, so that she gasped. "Kissing you..."

He bent, caressing her with his mouth until she began to burn. Somehow, they were back on the bed again, and his mouth was on her breasts, his hands adoring her while he brushed her silky skin with his lips.

"It won't...be enough," she moaned.

"My God, I know that," he said unsteadily.

He moved, easing his body over hers so that she could feel his arousal, his eyes holding hers as he caught his weight on his forearms and pressed his hips into hers.

"You'd let me, right now, wouldn't you?" he asked roughly.

"Yes." She let her hands learn the rigid muscles of his back, delighting in the slight roughness of his skin.

His mouth bent to hers and nibbled at her lower lip. "This is really stupid."

"I don't care. I belong to you."

He shuddered. The words went through him with incredible impact. He actually gasped.

"Well, I do," she whispered defensively. Her mouth opened under his. "Lift up, Harden."

He obeyed the soft whisper, feeling her hands suddenly between them. His shocked eyes met hers while she worked at the fastening of his belt. "My God, no!'' he burst out. He caught her hand and rolled onto his back, shivering.

She sat up, her eyes curious. "No?"

"You don't understand," he ground out.

Her soft eyes searched his face, seeing the restraint that was almost gone. "Oh. You mean that if I touch you that way, the same thing will happen to you that happened to me when...when you did it?"

"Yes." His cheeks went ruddy. He stared at her with desire and irritation and pain mingling. "I can't let you do that."

"Why?" she asked quietly.

"Call it an overdose of male pride," he muttered, and threw his long legs off the side of the bed. "Or a vicious hang-up. Call it whatever the hell you like, but I can't let you."

She watched him get to his feet and come around the bed, his eyes slow and quiet on her bare breasts as she sat watching him. "I let you," she pointed out.

"You're a woman." He drew in a jerky breath. "My God, you're all woman," he said huskily. "We'll set the bed on fire our first time."

She flushed. "You're avoiding the issue."

"Sure I am." He pulled her up, grabbed her knit top, and abruptly helped her back into it. "I'm an old-fashioned man with dozens of hang-ups—like being nude in front of a woman, like allowing myself to be satisfied with a woman seeing me helpless, like... Well, you get the idea, don't you?" he asked curtly. He shouldered into his shirt and caught her hand, tugging her along with him. "Feed me. I'm starving."

Her head whirled with the things she was learning about him as he led her into the kitchen. He was the most fascinating man she'd ever known. But she was beginning to wonder just how experienced he was. He didn't act like a ladies' man, even if he kissed like one.

The memory of the baby still nagged at the back of her mind. She was sorry about Tim, too, but as she went over and over the night of the wreck, she began to realize that no one could have done more than she had. She was an experienced driver, and a careful one. And Tim had been drinking. She couldn't have allowed him behind the wheel. The roads were slick, another car pulled out in front of her without warning, and she reacted instinctively, but a fraction of a second too late. It was fate. It had to be.

He watched her toy with her salad. "Brooding?" he asked gently.

She lifted her gray eyes to his and pushed back a long strand of disheveled dark hair. "Not really. I was thinking about the accident. I've been punishing myself for months, but the police said it was unavoidable, that there was nothing I could have done. They'd know, wouldn't they?"

"Yes," he told her gently. "They'd know."

"Tim wasn't good to me. All the same, I hate it that he died in such a way," she said sadly. "I regret losing my baby."

"I'll give you a baby," he said huskily, his pale eyes glittering with possession.

She looked up, surprised, straight into his face, and saw something that she didn't begin to understand. "You want children?" she asked softly.

His eyes fell to her breasts and back up to her mouth. "We're both dark haired. Your eyes are gray and mine are blue, and I'm darker skinned than you are. They'll probably favor both of us."

Her face brightened. "You...want a child with me?" she whispered.

He wondered about that wide-eyed delight. He knew she was still grieving for her child. If he could give her another one, it might help her to get over it. Even if she didn't love him, she might find some affection for him after the baby came. If he could get her pregnant. He knew that some men were sterile, and he'd never been tested. He didn't want to think about that possibility. He had to assume he could give her a child, for his own peace of mind. She was so terribly vulnerable. He found himself driven to protect her, to give her anything she needed to keep going.

"Yes," he said solemnly. "I want a child with you."

She beamed. Her eyes softened to the palest silver as they searched his hard face.

"But not right away," he said firmly. "First, you and I are going to do some serious socializing, get to know each other. There are a lot of hurdles we have to jump before we find a minister."

Meaning her marriage and her loss, she assumed. She managed a smile. "All right. Whatever you say, Harden."

He smiled back. Things were going better than he'd ever expected.

Miranda was nervous when he drove from the airport back to the Tremayne ranch. She barely heard what he said about the town and the landmarks they passed. His mother was an unknown quantity and she was half afraid of the first meeting. She'd seen Evan, his eldest brother, at the hotel, so he wouldn't be a stranger. But there were two other brothers, and both of them were married. She was all but holding her breath as Harden pulled the car onto the ranch road and eventually stopped in front of a white, two-story clapboard house.

"Don't fidget," Harden scolded gently, approving her white sundress with its colorful belt and her sexy high-heel sandals. "You look pretty and nobody here is going to savage you. All right?"

"All right," she said, but her eyes were troubled when he helped her out of the car.

Theodora Tremayne was hiding in the living room, peeking out of the curtains with Evan.

"He's brought a woman with him!" she burst out. "He's tormented me for years for what happened, first about his real father and then about that...that girl he loved." She closed her eyes. "He threatened once to bring me a prostitute, to get even, and that's what he's doing right now, isn't he, Evan? He's going to get even with me by bringing a woman of the streets into my home!"

Evan was too shocked to speak. By the time he finally realized that his mother knew nothing about Miranda, it was too late. He could even understand why she'd made such an assumption, because he'd heard Harden make the threat. Miranda was a city girl, and she dressed like one, with sophistication and style. Theodora, with her country background, could easily mistake a woman she didn't know for something she wasn't.

The front door opened and Miranda was marched into the living room by Harden.

"Miranda, this is my mother, Theodora," he said arrogantly, and without a word of greeting, which only cemented Theodora's horrified assumption.

Miranda stared at the small, dark woman who stood with clenched hands at her waist.

"It's . . . very nice to meet you," Miranda said, her voice shaking a little, because the older woman hadn't said a word or cracked a smile yet. She looked intimidating and furiously angry. Miranda's face flushed as she recognized the blatant hostility without understanding what had triggered it. "Harden's been kind to me . . ."

"I'll bet he has," Theodora said with uncharacteristic venom in her voice.

Miranda wasn't used to cruelty. She didn't quite know how to handle it. She swallowed down tears. "I . . . I guess I really should go, Harden," she blurted out, flushing violently as she met Harden's furious eyes. "I . . ."

"What kind of welcome is this?" he asked his mother.

"What kind did you expect?" Theodora countered, her eyes flashing. "This is a low-down thing to do to me, Harden."

"To you?" he growled. "How do you think Miranda feels?"

"I don't remember extending any invitations," Theodora replied stiffly.

Miranda was ready to get under the carpet. "Please, let's go," she appealed to Harden, almost frantic to leave.

"You just got here," Evan said shortly. "Come in and sit down, for God's sake."

But Miranda wouldn't budge. Her eyes pleaded with Harden.

He understood without a word being spoken. "All right, little one," he said gently. His hand slid down to take hers in a gesture of quiet comfort. "I'm sorry about this. We'll go."

"Nice to...to have met you," Miranda stammered, ready to run for it.

Harden was furious, and looked it. "Her husband was killed in a car wreck a few months back," he told his mother, watching her face stiffen with surprise. "She lost the baby she was carrying at the same time. I've been seeing her in Chicago, and I wanted her to visit Jacobsville. But considering the reception she just got, I don't imagine she'll miss the introductions."

He turned, his fingers caressing Miranda's, while Evan fumed and Theodora fought tears.

"Oh, no! No, please...!" Theodora spoke in a rush, embarrassed at her unkindness. The younger woman looked as if she'd been whipped, and despite Harden's lack of courtesy in telling her about this visit, she couldn't take it out on an innocent person. It was her own fault that she'd leaped to conclusions.

"I really have to go home," Miranda replied, her red face saying far more than the words. "My job...!"

Harden cursed under his breath. He brought her roughly to his side and held her there, his eyes protective as they went from her bowed head to his mother's tormented face.

"I asked Miranda down here to let her get to know my family and see if she likes it around here," he said with a cold smile. "Because if she does, I'm going to marry her. We can accomplish that without imposing on your hospitality," he told Theodora. "I'm sure the local motel has two rooms to spare."

Miranda looked up into Harden's face. "Don't," she said softly. "Please, don't. I shouldn't have come. Take me to the airport, please. I was wrong to come."

"No, you weren't," Evan said curtly. He glared at Theodora and then at Harden. "Look at her, damn it! Look what you're doing to her!"

Two pairs of eyes saw Miranda's white face, her huge, tragic eyes with their unnatural brightness.

"Evan's right," Theodora said with as much dignity as she could gather. "I'm sorry, Miranda. This isn't your fight."

"Which is why she's leaving," Harden added. He drew Miranda against him and turned her, gently maneuvering her out the door and back to the car.

"Where are you going?" Theodora asked miserably.

"Chicago," Harden said without breaking stride.

"She hasn't met Donald and Jo Ann, or Connal and Pepi," Evan remarked from the porch. He stuck his big hands into his pockets. "Not to mention that she hasn't had time to say hello to the bulls in the barn or learn to ride a horse, or especially, to get to know me. God knows, I'm the flower of the family."

Harden raised his eyebrows. "You?"

Evan glowered at him. "Me. I'm the eldest. After I was born, the rest of you were just an afterthought. You can't improve on perfection."

Miranda managed a smile at the banter. Evan was kind.

Theodora came down the steps and paused in front of her son and the other woman. "I've done this badly, and I'm sorry. You're very welcome in my home, Miranda. I'd like you to stay."

Miranda hesitated, looking up at Harden uncertainly.

"You'll never get to see all my sterling qualities if you leave now," Evan said.

She smiled involuntarily.

"And I just baked a chocolate cake," Theodora added with an unsteady smile. "And made a pot of coffee. You probably didn't have much to eat on the plane."

"We didn't," Miranda confessed. "I was too nervous to eat."

"Not without cause, either, it seems," Harden said with a glare at his mother.

"Cut it out, or we'll go for a walk behind the barn," Evan said with a smile that didn't touch his dark eyes. "Remember the last one?"

"You lost a tooth," Harden said.

"I was thinking about your broken nose," came the easy reply.

"You can't fight," Theodora told them. "Miranda probably already thinks she's been landed in a brawl. We should be able to be civil to each other if we try."

"For a few days, anyway," Evan agreed. "Don't worry, honey, I'll protect you from them," he said in a stage whisper.

She did laugh, then, at the wicked smile on his broad face. She clung to Harden's hand and went back into the house.

Theodora was less brittle after they'd had coffee, but it wasn't until Evan took Harden off to see some new cattle that she really warmed up.

"I'm sorry about all his," she told Miranda earnestly. "Harden...likes to make things difficult for me, you see. I didn't know you were coming with him."

Miranda paled. "He didn't tell you?!"

Theodora grimaced. "Oh, dear. You didn't know, did you? I feel even worse now." She didn't, couldn't add, that she'd thought Miranda was a woman of the streets. That tragic young face was wounded enough without adding insult to injury.

"I'm so sorry...I can get a room in the motel," she began almost frantically.

Theodora laid a gentle hand on her arm. "Don't. Now that Donald and Jo Ann have their own home, like Connal and Pepi, I never have much female company. I'll enjoy having someone to talk to." She studied Miranda's wan face. "Harden's never brought a woman home."

"He feels sorry for me," Miranda said bluntly. "And he wants me." Her thin shoulders rose and fell. "I don't know why he wants to marry me, really, but he's relentless, isn't he? I was on the plane before I knew it."

Theodora smiled. "Yes, he's relentless. And he can be cruel." She drew in a steadying breath. "I can't pretend that he doesn't have a reason for that. I...had an affair. Harden was the result."

"Yes, I know." She replied, her voice gentle. "He told me."

Theodora's eyes widened. "That's a first! I don't think he's ever told anyone else."

"I suppose he isn't on his guard so much with me," Miranda said. "You see, I haven't had much spirit since the accident."

"It must have been terrible for you. You loved your husband?" she asked.

"I was fond of him," Miranda corrected. "And sorry that he had to die the way he did. It's my baby that I miss the most. I wanted him so much!"

"I lost two," Theodora said quietly. "I understand. Time will help."

Miranda's eyes narrowed as she looked at the older woman. "Forgive me, but it's more than just the circumstances of Harden's birth between the two of you, isn't it?" she asked very gently. "There's something more..."

Theodora caught her breath. "You're very perceptive, my dear. Yes, there is something more."

"I don't mean to pry," Miranda said when Theodora hesitated.

"No. It's your right to know. I'm not sure that Harden would ever talk about it." She leaned forward. "There was a girl. They were very much in love, but her parents disapproved. They had planned to elope and get married." Theodora's eyes went dull and sad with the memory. "She called here one night, frantic, begging to speak to Harden." She grimaced. "He'd gone to bed, and I thought they'd had a quarrel or something and it could wait until morning. Harden and I have never been really close, so I knew nothing of their plans to elope, or even that he was honestly in love with her. She seemed to be forever calling at bad times. I was trying to finish up in the kitchen because it was late, and I was tired. I lied. I told her that he didn't want to talk to her at the moment, and I hung up."

Miranda frowned slightly, not understanding.

Theodora looked up. "Her parents had found out about the elopement and were making arrangements to send her to a school in Switzerland to get her away from Harden. I can only guess that having Harden refuse to speak to her, as I made it sound, was the last straw. She walked out onto the second-story balcony of her house and jumped off, to the stone patio below. She died instantly."

Miranda's eyes closed as she pictured how it would have been for Harden after that. He was sensitive, and deep, and to lose someone he'd loved that much because of a thoughtless phone call must have taken all the color out of his world.

"Yes, you understand, don't you?" Theodora asked quietly. "He stayed drunk for weeks afterward." She dabbed at tears. "I've never forgiven myself, either. It was twelve years ago, but it might as well have been yesterday as far as Harden is concerned. That, added to the circumstances of his birth, has made me his worst enemy and turned him against women with a vengeance."

"I'm sorry, for both of you," Miranda said. "It can't have been an easy thing to get over."

Theodora sipped coffee before she spoke. "As you see, Miranda, we all have our crosses," she mused.

"Yes." She picked up her own coffee cup. "Thank you for telling me."

Theodora's eyes narrowed. "Do you love him?"

The younger woman's face flushed, but she didn't look away. "With all my heart," she said. It was the first time she'd admitted it, even to herself.

"Harden is very protective of you," Theodora observed. "And he seems to be serious."

"He wants me very badly," Miranda said. "But whether or not he feels anything else, only he knows. Desire isn't enough, really."

"Love can grow out of it, though. Harden knows how to love. He's just forgotten." Theodora smiled. "Perhaps you can reeducate him."

Miranda smiled back. "Perhaps. You're sure you don't mind if I stay with you? I was serious about the motel."

"I'm very sure, Miranda." Theodora watched the young face relax, and she was glad she hadn't made the situation worse than it was.

Evan and Harden were on their way back to the house before Evan said anything about Miranda's arrival.

"I can't believe you brought her home," he murmured, grinning at his younger brother. "People will faint all over Jacobsville if you get married."

Harden shrugged. "She's young and pretty, and we get along. It's time I married someone." His eyes ran slowly around the property. "Even if there are four of us, we'll need sons to help us keep the place. I'd hate to see it cut up into subdivisions one day."

"So would I." Evan shoved his big hands into his pockets. "Mother thought you were bringing that streetwalker you threatened her with once. Not that I expect you'd know a streetwalker if you saw one," he murmured dryly, "considering your years of celibacy."

Harden let the insinuation go, as he always did, but he frowned. "You didn't tell Theodora who Miranda was?"

"I started to, but there wasn't time." His expression sobered. "You should have called first. No matter what vendettas you're conducting against Mother, you owe her a little common courtesy. Presenting her with a houseguest and no advance notice is unforgivable."

Harden, surprisingly, agreed. "Yes, I know." He broke off a twig from the low-hanging limb of one of the pecan trees as they passed through the small orchard and toyed with it. "Has Theodora ever talked about my real father?" he asked suddenly.

Chapter Eight

Evan's eyebrows shot up and he stopped walking. Harden had never once asked anything about his real father. He hadn't even wanted to know the man's name.

"What brought on that question?" he asked.

Harden frowned. "I don't know. I'm just curious. I'd like to know something about him, that's all."

"You'll have to ask Mother, then," Evan told him. "Because she's the only one who can tell you what you want to know."

He grimaced. "Wouldn't she love that?" he asked darkly.

Evan turned. "She'll die one day," he said shortly. "You're going to have to live with the way you treat her."

Harden looked dangerous for a minute, but his eyes calmed. He stared out over the land. "Yes, I know," he confessed. "But she's got some things to deal with herself."

"I have a simpler philosophy than you," Evan said quietly. "I believe that the day we die is preordained. That being the case, I can accept tragedy a little better than you can. If you think Theodora played God that night, think again. You of all people should know that nobody can interfere if God wants someone to live."

Harden's heart jumped. He scowled, but he didn't speak.

"Hadn't considered that, had you?" Evan asked. "You've been so eaten up with hatred and vengeance that you haven't even thought about God's hand in life. You're the churchgoer, not me. Why don't you try living what you preach? Let's see a little forgiveness, or isn't that what your religion is supposed to be all about?"

He walked ahead of Harden to the house, leaving the other man quiet and thoughtful.

Supper that evening was boisterous. Donald and Jo Ann were live wires, vying with Evan for wisecracks, and they made up for Harden's brooding and Theodora's discomfort.

Donald was shorter and more wiry than his brothers, although he had dark hair and eyes like Evan. Jo Ann was redheaded and blue-eyed, a little doll with a ready smile and a big heart. They took to Miranda at once, and she began to feel more at home by the minute, despite Harden's lack of enthusiasm for the gathering.

After the meal, Harden excused himself and went outside. He didn't ask Miranda to join him, but she did.

He glanced back at her, startled. "I thought you were having the time of your life with the family."

She smiled at his belligerence. It was uncanny, how well she understood him. He was the outsider; he didn't fit in. He was on his guard and frankly jealous of the attention she was getting from the family he pretended he wasn't a part of. She couldn't let on that she knew that, of course.

She moved to join him on the porch swing, where he was lazily smoking a cigarette.

"I like your family very much," she agreed. "But I came here because of you."

He was touched. He hadn't been wrong about her after all. She seemed to know things about him, emotionally, that he couldn't manage to share with her in words.

Hesitantly he slid his free arm around her and drew her close, loving the way she clung, her hand resting warmly over his chest while the swing creaked rhythmically on its chains.

"It's so peaceful here," she said with a sigh.

"Too peaceful for you, city girl?" he teased gently.

She started to tell him about her background, but she decided to keep her secret for a little longer. He had to want her for herself, not just because she could fit in on a ranch. She didn't want to prejudice his decision about marrying her until she was sure of his feelings.

"I travel a good deal. And I'll keep the apartment in Houston. You won't get too bored," he promised her. He stared at her dark head with new possession. "Lift your face, Miranda," he said, his voice soft and deep in the quiet. "I'm going to kiss you."

She obeyed him without conscious thought, waiting for his mouth. It was smoky from the cigarette, and still warm from the coffee he'd had with supper. But most of all, it was slow, and a little rough, and very thorough.

A soft moan broke the silence. She lifted her arms, startled by the onrush of passion that made her desperate for more of him than this.

If she felt it, so did he. The cigarette went over the banister as he lifted her across him, and the kiss went from a slow exploration to a statement of intent in seconds.

She heard him curse under his breath as he fought the buttons of her shirtwaist dress, and then his hand was on her, possessive in its caressing warmth.

"Miranda," he whispered into her mouth. His hand was faintly tremulous where it traced the swollen contours of her breast.

He lifted his head and drew the dress away from her body, but the porch was too dark to suit him. He stood up with Miranda in his arms and moved toward the settee against the wall, where the light from the living room filtered through the curtains onto the porch.

"Where are we going?" Miranda asked, dazed by the force of her own desire.

"Into the light," he said huskily, "I have to see you." He sat down with Miranda in his arms, turning her so that he could see her breasts. "I have to look at you...Yes!"

"Harden?" She barely recognized her own high-pitched voice, so shaken was she by the look on his face.

"You're beautiful, little one," he whispered, meeting her eyes. His hand moved and she shivered. His head bent to her mouth, brushing it tenderly. "Do you have any idea what you do to me?"

"The same thing you do to me, I hope," she whispered. Her body arched helplessly. "Harden," she moaned. "Someone could come out here. Oh, can't we go somewhere...?"

He caught his breath and looked around almost desperately. "Yes." He got up and buttoned her deftly back into her dress, only to catch her hand and lead her along with him. His mind was barely working at all. Nowhere in the house was safe, with that crowd. Neither was the barn, because two calving heifers were in there, being closely watched as they prepared to drop purebred calves.

His eyes found his car, and he sighed with resignation as he drew Miranda toward it. He put her inside and climbed in with her, turning her into his arms the instant the door was closed.

"Now," he breathed against her waiting mouth.

He unbuttoned the dress again and found her with his hands, and then with his mouth. Her arms clung to him, loving the newness of being with him like this, of enjoying physical intimacy. She slid her hands inside his shirt and found the hard, hair-roughened warmth of his chest, liking the way he responded to her searching touch.

"Here," he said curtly, unfastening the shirt all the way down. He gathered her to him inside it, pressing her soft breasts into the hard muscles of his chest. He lifted his head and looked down at where they touched, at the contrasts, in the light that glared out of the barn window.

He moved her away just a little, so that he could see the hard tips of her breasts barely touching him, their deep mauve dusky against his tanned skin. His forefinger touched her there, and his blue eyes lifted to her silvery ones when she gasped.

"Why do you... watch me like that?" she whispered.

"I enjoy the way you look when I touch you," he said softly. "Your eyes glow, like silver in sunlight." His gaze went to her swollen mouth, down her creamy throat to her breasts. "Your body... colors, like your cheeks, when I touch you intimately. Each time is like the first time you've known a man's lovemaking. That's why."

"It's the first time I ever felt like this," she replied. "It always embarrassed me with Tim. I felt... inadequate." she searched his narrow eyes. He looked very sensuous with his shirt unbuttoned and his hair disheveled by her hands. "I've never been embarrassed with you."

"It's natural, isn't it?" he asked quietly. "Like breathing." His forefinger began to trace the hard nipple and she clutched his shirt and shuddered.

"Addictive and dangerous," he whispered as his mouth hovered over hers and his touch grew more sensual, more arousing. "Like . . . loving . . ."

His mouth covered hers before she could be certain that she'd heard the word at all, and then it was too late to think. She gave him her mouth, all of her body that he wanted, abandoned and passionately in love, totally without shame.

"No, don't!" she wept frantically when he pulled back.

He stilled her hands and drew her close, rocking her against him. He was shivering, too, and his voice was strained. "I hurt, little one," he whispered. "Be still. Let me calm down."

She bit her lower lip until she almost drew blood, trembling in his arms. He whispered to her, soothed her with his voice and his hands until she calmed and lay still against him, trying to breathe.

He let out a long breath. "My God, it's been a long time since I've been that excited by a woman. A few more seconds and I couldn't have pulled back at all."

She nuzzled her face into his hot throat. "Would it be the end of the world if we went all the way?" she whispered boldly.

"No. Probably not. But as my brother Evan reminded me about something else tonight, it's time I started practicing what I preach. I want a ring on your finger before I make love to you completely."

"You're a hopeless Puritan," she murmured dryly.

"Yes, I am," he agreed. He raised his cheek from her dark hair. "And a pretty desperate one. Name a date."

She stared at him worriedly. She was sure. But it was his body that wanted her most, not his heart. "Harden, you have to be sure."

"I'm sure."

"I know how badly you want me," she began, frowning uncertainly. "But there has to be more than just that."

He didn't listen. He was looking down his nose at her with glittery blue eyes. "You can have two weeks to make up your mind."

"And, after that?" she asked slowly.

"After that, I'll pick you up, fly you down to Mexico, and you'll be married before you have time to argue about it."

"That's not fair!" she exclaimed.

"I don't feel fair," he shot back. "My God, I'm alive, really alive, for the first time in my life, and so are you. I'm not going to let you throw this away."

"But what if it's all just physical?" she groaned.

"Then it's still more than four out of five couples have. You'll get used to me. I won't pretend that it's going to be easy, but you will. I'll never lift a hand to you, or do anything to shame you. I won't stifle you as a person. All I'll expect from you is fidelity. And later, perhaps, a child."

"I'd like to have a family," she said quietly. She lowered her eyes. "I suppose sometimes we do get second chances, don't we?"

He'd been thinking the same thing. His fingers touched her cheek, smoothing down to her mouth. "Yes. Sometimes we do, Miranda." He brushed her lips gently with his before he rearranged their disheveled clothing and led her back to the house.

Miranda felt like an actress playing a part for the next few days. Determined to find out if Harden could accept her as he thought she was, she played the city ingenue to the hilt. Leaving the jeans and cotton shirts she'd packed still in their cases, she chose her best dress slacks—white ones, of course—and silk blouses to wear around the ranch. She did her makeup as carefully as if she were going to work. She acted as if she found the cattle smelly and frightening.

"They won't hurt you," Harden said, and it was taking a real effort not to react badly to this side of her. He didn't know what he'd expected, but it wasn't to find her afraid of cattle. That was a bad omen. Worse, she balked when he offered to take her riding.

"I don't like horses," she lied. "I've only been on them once or twice, and it's uncomfortable and scary. Can't we go in the truck?"

Harden had to bite his tongue. "Of course, we can," he said with gentlemanly courtesy. "It doesn't matter."

It did, though, she could tell. She clung to his arm as they walked back from the barn, because she was wearing high heels.

"Honey, don't you have some less dressy slacks and some flat shoes?" he asked after a minute, frowning down at her. "That's really not the rig to wear around here. You'll ruin your pretty things."

She smiled at the consideration and pressed closer. "I don't care. I love being with you."

His arm slid around her, and all his worries about her ability to fit in disappeared like fog in sunlight. "I like being with you, too," he said quietly. He held her against his side, aware of mingled feelings of peace and riotous desire and pleasure as he felt her softness melt into his strength so trustingly.

"It bothers you, doesn't it, that I'm not a country girl?" she asked when they reached the truck.

He frowned. His pale blue eyes searched her gray ones. "It isn't that important," he said stubbornly. "After all, you won't be expected to help me herd cattle or pull calves. We have other common interests."

"Yes. Like walks in the park and science fiction movies and quiet nights at home watching television," she said, grinning up at him.

The frown didn't fade. He couldn't put it into words, but it was a little surprising that a woman who liked the park and loathed parties wouldn't be right at home on a ranch.

He shrugged it off and put her into the cab of the truck beside him, driving around to where Old Man Red, their prize-winning Santa Gertrudis bull lived in air-conditioned luxury in his own barn.

Miranda had to stifle a gasp of pure pleasure when she saw the enormous animal. He had the most beautiful conformation she'd ever seen, and she'd seen plenty in her childhood and adolescence on her father's South Dakota ranch. She knew Old Man Red's name from the livestock sale papers, from the annual breeders' editions. He was a legend in cattle circles, and here he stood, close enough to touch. His progeny thrived not only in the United States, but in countries around the world.

"He's so big," she said, sighing with unconscious delight.

"Our pride and joy," Harden replied. He reached out and smoothed the animal's muzzle affectionately. "He's been cosseted so much that he's nothing but a big pet these days."

"An expensive one, I'll bet," she said, trying not to give away her own knowledge of his value.

"He is that." He looked down at her. "I thought you didn't like cattle, city girl," he murmured. "Your eyes sure sparkle when you look at him."

She reached up to his ear. "Roast beef," she whispered. "I'm drooling."

"You cannibal!" he burst out, and laughed.

The sound was new, and pleasant. Startled, she laughed, too. "I'm sorry. That was unforgivable, wasn't it?" she mused.

"I'd rather eat my older brother Evan than put a fork to Old Man Red!"

Her eyebrows went up. "Poor Evan!"

"No, poor me," he replied. "He'd probably take weeks of tenderizing just to be digestible."

She slid her fingers into his and followed him down the wide aisle of the barn, happier than she could ever remember being. "Did you grow up here?"

He nodded. "My brothers and I used to play cowboy and Indian."

"You always got to be the Indian," she imagined.

He frowned. "How did you know that?"

"You're stoic," she said simply. "Very dignified and aloof."

"So is Connal. You'll meet him tonight. He's bringing Pepi and the baby over." He hesitated, staring at her expression. "It's going to hurt, isn't it?"

She turned, looking up at him. "Not if you're with me."

His breath caught. She made him feel so necessary. He caught her by the arms and drew her slowly to him, enfolding her. He laid his cheek against her dark hair and the wind blew down the long aisle, bringing the scent of fresh hay and cattle with it.

"I suppose you played with dolls when you were a little girl," he murmured.

"Not really. I liked to—" She stopped dead, because she couldn't admit, just yet, that she was riding in rodeos when she was in grammar school. Winning trophies, too. Thank God Sam had kept those at his house, so Harden hadn't seen them when he came to her apartment.

"You liked to...?" he prompted.

"Play dress-up in mother's best clothes," she invented.

"Girl stuff," he murmured. "I liked Indian leg wrestling and chasing lizards and snakes."

"Yuuck!" she said eloquently.

"Snakes are beneficial," he replied. "They eat the mice that eat up our grain."

"If you say so."

He tilted her face up to his dancing eyes. "Tenderfoot," he accused, but he made it sound like a caress.

"You'd be happier with a country girl, wouldn't you?" she asked softly. "Someone who could ride and liked cattle."

He drew in a slow, even breath and let his eyes wander slowly over the gentle oval of her face. "We don't get to pick and choose the qualities and abilities that make up a person. Your inner qualities are much more important to me than any talent you might have had for horseback riding. You're loyal and honest and compassionate, and in my arms, you burn. That's enough." He scowled. "Am I enough for you, though?"

"What a question!" she exclaimed, touched by the way he'd described her.

"I'm hard and unsociable. I don't go to parties and I don't pull my punches with people. There are times when being alone is like a religion to me. I find it difficult to share things, feelings." His broad shoulders lifted and fell, and he looked briefly worried. "Added to that, I've been down on women for so many years it isn't even funny. You may find me tough going."

She searched his eyes quietly. "You didn't even like me when we first met, but you came after me when you thought I might be suicidal. You looked after me and you never asked for anything." She smiled gently. "Mr. Tremayne, I knew everything I needed to know about you after just twenty-four hours."

He bent and brushed his mouth over her eyelids with breathless tenderness. "What if I fail you?" he whispered.

"What if I fail you?" she replied. She savored the touch of his mouth on her face, keenly aware of the rising tide of heat in her blood as his hands began to move up her back. "I'm a city girl...."

His breath grew unsteady. "I don't care," he said roughly. His mouth began to search for hers, hard and insistent. His hands went to her hips and jerked them up into his. "My God, I don't care what you are!" His mouth crushed down against her parted lips, and his last sane thought was that she was every bit as wild for him as he was for her.

Heated seconds later, she felt his mouth lift and her eyes opened slowly, dazed.

"Harden," she breathed.

His teeth delicately caught her upper lip and traced it. "Did I hurt you?" he whispered.

"No." Her arms linked around his neck and she lay against him heavily, her heartbeat shaking her, her eyes closed.

"We can live in Houston," he said unsteadily. "Maybe someday you'll learn to like the ranch. If you don't, it doesn't matter."

Her mind registered what he was saying, but before she could respond to it, his mouth was on hers again, and she forgot everything....

Connal and his wife, Pepi, came that night. They brought along their son, Jamie, who immediately became the center of attention.

Pepi didn't know about Miranda's lost baby, because nobody had told her. But she noticed a sad, wistful look on the other woman's face when she looked at the child.

"Something's wrong," she said softly, touching Miranda's thin hand while the men gathered to talk cattle and Theodora was helping Jeanie May in the kitchen. "What is it?"

Miranda told her, finding something gentle and very special in the other woman's brown eyes.

"I'm sorry," Pepi said afterward. "But you'll have other babies. I know you will."

"I hope so," Miranda replied, smiling. Involuntarily her eyes went to Harden.

"Connal says he's never brought a woman home before," Pepi said. "There was something about an engagement years ago, although I never found out exactly what. I know that Harden hates Theodora, and he's taken it out on every woman who came near him. Until now," she added, her big eyes searching Miranda's. "You must be very special to him."

"I hope I am," Miranda said earnestly. "I don't know. It's sort of like a trial period. We're getting to know each other before he decides when we'll get married.

"Oh. So it's like that," Pepi said, grinning.

"He's a bulldozer."

"All the Tremayne brothers are, even Donald, you just ask Jo Ann." Pepi laughed. "I used to be scared to death of Harden myself, but he set me right about Connal once and maybe saved my marriage."

"He can be so intimidating," Miranda agreed. "Evan's the only even-tempered one, from what I see."

"Get Harden to tell you about the time Evan threw one of the cowboys over a fence," Pepi chuckled. "It's an eye-opener. Evan's deep, and not quite what he seems."

"He's friendly, at least," Miranda said.

"If he likes you. I hear he can be very difficult if he doesn't. Don't you love Theodora?"

"Yes, I do," Miranda replied. "We got off to a rocky start. Harden brought me down without warning Theodora first, but she warmed up after we were properly introduced. I'm enjoying it, now."

Pepi frowned. "I thought you didn't like ranch life."

"I'm getting used to it, I think."

"You'll like it better when you learn to ride," the other woman promised. "I hear Harden's going to teach you how."

Miranda's silver eyes opened wide. "He is?" she asked with assumed innocence.

"Yes. You'll enjoy it, I know you will. Horses are terrific."

"So I hear."

"Just never let them know you're afraid of them, and you'll do fine." The baby cried suddenly, and Pepi smiled down at him, her eyes soft with love. "Hungry, little boy?" she asked tenderly. "Miranda, could you hold him while I dig out his bottle?"

"Oh, of course!" came the immediate reply.

Pepi went to heat the bottle, and Miranda sighed over the tiny laughing face, her own mirroring her utter delight.

She wasn't aware of Harden's stare until he knelt beside her and touched a tiny little hand with one big finger.

"Isn't he beautiful?" Miranda asked, her eyes finding his.

He nodded. His eyes darkened, narrowed. His body burned with sudden need. "Do you want me to give you a child, Miranda?" he asked huskily.

Her face colored. Her lips parted. Her soft eyes searched his and linked with them in the silence that followed.

"Yes," she said unsteadily.

His eyes flashed, glittering down at her. "Then you'd better make up your mind to marry me, hadn't you?"

"Admiring your nephew?" Pepi asked as she joined them, breaking the spell.

"He's the image of Connal," Harden mused.

"Isn't he, though?" Pepi sighed, smiling toward her husband, who returned the look with breathless tenderness.

"Stop that," Harden muttered. "You people have been married over a year."

"It gets better every day," Pepi informed him. She grinned. "You ought to try it."

"I want to, if I could get my intended to agree," he murmured dryly, watching Miranda closely. "She's as slow as molasses about making up her mind."

"And you're impatient," she accused him.

"Can't help it," he replied. "It isn't every day that a man runs across a girl like you. I don't want Evan to snap you up."

"Did you mention my name?" Evan asked, grinning as he towered over them. "Nice job, Pepi," he said. "Now, how about a niece?"

"Don't rush me," she said. "I'm just getting used to making formula."

"You're a natural. Look at the smile on that little face."

"Why don't you get married and have kids?" Connal asked the eldest Tremayne as he sauntered over to the small group.

Evan's expression closed up. "I told you once, they trample me trying to get to him." He stuck a finger toward Harden.

"They'll have to get past Miranda now, though," Connal replied. "Harden will go on the endangered species list."

"Evan has been on it for years," Harden chuckled. "Except that Anna can't convince him she's serious competition."

"I don't rob cradles," Evan said coldly. His dark eyes glittered, and his usual good nature went into eclipse, giving a glimpse of the formidable man behind the smiling mask.

"Your mother was nineteen when she married, wasn't she?" Pepi asked him.

"That was back in the dark ages."

"You might as well give up," Connal said, sliding a possessive arm around his wife as he smiled down at her. "He's worse than Harden was."

"Meaning that Harden is improving?" Evan asked, forcing a smile. He studied Harden closely. "You know, he is. He's actually been pleasant since he's been home this time. A nice change," he told Miranda, "from his first few days home from Chicago, when he took rust off old nails with his tongue and caused two wranglers to quit on the spot.''

"He was horrible,'' Connal agreed. "Mother asked if she could go and live with Donald and Jo Ann.''

Evan chuckled. "Then she took back the offer because I threatened to load my gun. She's fonder of Harden than she is of the rest of us.''

Harden's face went taut. "That's enough.''

Evan shrugged. "It's no big family secret that you're her favorite,'' he reminded the other man. "It's your sweet nature that stole her heart.''

Once, Harden would have swung on his brother for that remark. Now, he actually smiled. "She should have hit you harder while she had the chance.''

"I grew too fast,'' Evan said imperturbably.

"Are you sure you've stopped yet?'' Connal mused, looking up at the other man.

Evan didn't answer him. His size was his sore spot, and Connal had been away long enough to forget. He turned back to Harden. "Did you ever get in touch with Scarborough about that shipment that got held up in Fort Worth?''

"Yes, I did,'' Harden said. "It's all ironed out now.''

"That's a relief.''

The men drifted back to business talk, and Pepi and Miranda played with the baby until Theodora rejoined them. Dinner was on the table shortly, and all the solemnity died out of the occasion. Miranda couldn't remember when she'd enjoyed anything more.

Harden noticed how easily she fit in with his family, and it pleased him. She might not be the ideal ranch wife, but she was special, and he wanted her. They'd have a good marriage. They'd make it work. But one thing he did mean to do, and that was to show Miranda how to ride a horse. Tomorrow, he promised himself. Tomorrow, he was going to ease her onto a tame horse and coax her to ride with him. Once she learned how, she was going to love it. That would get one hurdle out of the way.

The rest would take care of themselves. He watched Miranda with an expression that would have knocked the breath out of her if she'd seen it. The flickering lights in his pale blue eyes were much more than infatuation or physical interest. They were the beginnings of something deep and poignant and real.

Chapter Nine

The next morning, Harden knocked on her door earlier than he had since they'd been at the ranch.

"Get up and put on some jeans and boots and a cotton shirt," he called. "If you don't have any, we'll borrow some of Jo Ann's for you—she's about your size."

"I've got some," she called back. "What are you up to?"

"I'm going to teach you to ride. Come on down to the stables when you finish breakfast. I've got to go and get the men started."

"Okay," she called with silent glee. "I'd just love to learn how to ride!"

"Good. Hurry up, honey."

His booted footsteps died away, and Miranda laughed delightedly as she dressed. Now that he was ready to accept the city girl he thought she was, it was time to let him in on the truth. It was, she anticipated, going to be delicious!

It was like going back in time for Miranda, who was right at home in jeans and boots and a red-checked cotton shirt. Harden met her at the stables, where he already had two horses saddled.

"You look cute," he said, grinning at the ponytail. "Almost like a cowgirl."

And you ain't seen nothin' yet, cowboy, she was thinking. "I'm glad I look the part," she said brightly. "What do we do first?"

"First, you learn how to mount. Now, there's nothing to be afraid of," he assured her. "This is the gentlest horse on the place. I'll lead you through the basics. Anyone can learn to ride. All you have to do is pay attention and do what I tell you."

He made it sound as if she'd never seen a horse. Of course, he knew nothing about her past, but still, her pride began to sting as he went through those basics in a faintly condescending tone.

"The hardest part is getting on the horse," he concluded. "But there's nothing to it, once you know how. It'll only take a minute to teach you the right way to do it."

"Oh, I'd love to learn the right way to get on a horse!" she exclaimed with mock enthusiasm. "Uh, would you hold the reins a minute?" she asked with twinkling eyes.

"Sure." He frowned as he took them. "What for?"

"You'll see." She walked away from him, trying not to double up with mischievous laughter as she thought about what she was going to do.

"Got him?" she called when she was several yards away.

"I've got him," he said impatiently. "What in hell do you want me to do with him?"

"Just hold him, while I show you how I've *been* getting on horses." She got her bearings and suddenly took off toward the horse at a dead run. She jumped, balanced briefly on her hands on the horse's rump, and vaulted into the saddle as cleanly and neatly as she'd done it in rodeos years ago.

The look on Harden's face was worth money. Evan had been standing nearby, and he saw it, too, but he didn't look as if he trusted his eyes.

Miranda shook back her ponytail and laughed delightedly. "Gosh, you look strange," she told Harden.

"You didn't tell me you could do that!" he burst out.

She shrugged. "Nothing to it. I took first prizes in barrel racing back in South Dakota, and Dad used to say I was the best horseman he had on the place."

"What place?" he asked explosively.

"His ranch," she replied. She grinned at his shell-shocked expression. "Well, you're the one who said I was a city girl, weren't you?"

Harden's face wavered and broke into the most beautiful smile she'd ever seen. His blue eyes beamed up at her with admiration and pride and something more, something soft and elusive.

"Full of surprises, aren't you?" he asked, laying a lean hand on her thigh.

"I reckon I am," she chuckled. "Got a hat I can borrow?"

"Here." Evan tossed her one, barely concealing a chuckle. "My, my, they must have lots of horses in Chicago. You sure do look experienced at getting on them."

"She's a South Dakota ranch girl," Harden told him dryly. "Nice of her to share that tidbit, wasn't it?"

"Noting like the element of surprise," Miranda said smugly, putting the oversize hat on. She glowered at Evan with it covering her ears. "If you'll get me a handle, I can use it for an umbrella."

Evan glared at her. "I do not have a big head."

"Oh, no, of course not," she agreed, flopping the hat back and forth on her head. She grinned at Evan.

"Okay," Evan said. "I'll relent enough to admit that you have a very small head."

"How long have you been riding?" Harden asked her.

"Since I was three," she confessed. "I still go riding in Chicago. I love horses."

"Can you cut cattle?" he persisted.

"If you put me on a trained quarter horse, you bet," she replied. "With all due respect, this rocking horse isn't going to be much good in a herd of cattle."

Harden chuckled. "No, he's not. I'll saddle Dusty for you. Then we'll go work for a while."

"Surprise, surprise," Evan murmured as he joined his brother.

"The biggest hurdle of all was her city upbringing," Harden said with pure glee. "And she turns out to be a cowgirl."

"That lady's one of a kind," Evan mused. "Don't lose her."

"No chance. Not if I have to tie her to the bedpost."

Evan gave him a dry look. "Kinky, are you?"

Harden glared at him and strode off into the barn.

For the next three days, Miranda discovered more in common with Harden than she'd ever imagined. But in the back of her mind, always, was the woman he'd loved and lost. He couldn't be over her if he still held such a bitter grudge against his mother. While his heart was tangled up, he couldn't love anyone else. And if he didn't love her, their marriage would have very little chance of success.

She watched Harden work on one of the purebred mares in foal, fascinated by the tenderness with which he helped the mare through her ordeal. For all his faults, when the chips were down, he was the coolest, most compassionate man she'd ever known. In an emergency, he'd be a good man to have around.

"One more week," he reminded her when he was through with the mare. "Then I'll take the decision right out of your hands."

"You can't force me to marry you," she said stubbornly.

His eyes ran down her body with possession and barely controlled desire. "Watch me."

"I'd have to be out of my mind to marry you," she exploded. "I couldn't call my soul my own!"

He lifted his head and smiled at her arrogantly, his pale eyes glittery. "I'll have you, all the same. And you'll like it."

"You arrogant, unprincipled, overbearing—"

"Save it up, honey," he interrupted, jerking his hat down over one eyebrow. "I've got a man waiting on a cattle deal."

He dropped a hard kiss on her open mouth and left her standing, fuming, behind him.

Harden had given her permission to ride any of his horses except an oversize, bad-tempered stallion named Rocket. Normally, she wouldn't have gone against him. But he was acting like the Supreme Male, and she didn't like it. She saddled the stallion and took him out, riding hell for leather until she and the horse were too tired to go any farther.

She paused to water him at a small stream, talking to him gently. His reputation was largely undeserved, because he was a gentle horse as long as he had a firm hand. In many ways, he and she were kindred spirits. She'd left behind her unbridled youth, and Tim had made her uncomfortable with her femininity. She'd felt like a thing during most of her marriage, a toy that Tim took off the shelf when he was bored. But with Harden, she felt wild and rebellious. He brought all her buried passions to the surface, and some of them were uncomfortable.

When she glanced at her watch, she was surprised to find how much time had elapsed since she'd taken Rocket out of the barn. At a guess, she was going to be in a lot of trouble when she got back.

Sure enough, Harden was marching around the front of the barn, a cigarette in his hand, his normally lazy stride converted into a quick, impatient pacing. Even the set of his head was dangerous.

Miranda got out of the saddle and led Rocket the rest of the way. Her jeans were splattered with mud, like her boots, and her yellow cotton shirt wasn't much cleaner. Her hair, pinned up in a braid, was untidy. But her face was alive as never before, flushed with exhilaration, her gray eyes bright with challenge and excitement.

Harden turned and stiffened as she approached. Evan was nearby, probably to save her from him, she thought mischievously.

"Here," she said, handing him the reins. She lifted her face, daring him. "Go ahead. Yell. Shout. Curse. Give me hell."

His face was hard and his eyes were glittery, but he did none of those things. Unexpectedly he jerked her into his arms and stood holding her, a faint tremor in his lean, fit body as he held hers against it.

The action shocked her out of all resistance, because it told her graphically how worried he'd been. The shock of it took the edge off her temper, made her relax against him with pure delight.

"I forgot the time," she said at his ear. "I didn't do it on purpose." She clung to him, her eyes closed. "I'm sorry you were worried."

"How do you know I was?" he asked curtly.

She smiled into his warm neck. "I don't know. But I do." Her arms tightened. "Going to kiss me?" she whispered.

"I'd kiss you blind if my brother wasn't standing ten feet away trying to look invisible. That being the case, it will have to wait." He lifted his head. His face was paler than usual. "Monday, we're getting married. I can't take anymore. Either you marry me, or you get out of my life."

She searched his eyes. It would be taking a huge chance. But she'd learned that they were pretty compatible, and she knew he was beginning to feel something besides physical attraction for her. At least, she hoped he was. They got along well together. She knew and enjoyed ranch life, so there wouldn't be much adjustment in that quarter. Anyway, the alternative was going back to Chicago to live with her ghosts and try to live without Harden. She'd tried that once and failed. She wasn't strong enough to try it again. She smiled up at him softly. "Monday, then," she said quietly.

Harden hadn't realized that he'd been holding his breath. He let it out slowly, feeling as if he'd just been handed the key to the world. He looked down at her. "Good enough. But just for the record, honey, if you ever, ever, get on that horse again without permission," he said in a seething undertone, "I'll feed him to you, tail first!"

She lifted her eyebrows. "You and whose army, buster?"

He grinned. He chuckled. He wrapped her up and gave her a bear hug, the first really affectionate gesture of their turbulent relationship.

They were married the following Monday. Miranda's brother, Sam, gave her away, and Evan was best man.

Joan, Sam's wife, managed to get a radiant Miranda alone long enough to find out how happy she really was.

"No more looking back," Joan said softly. "Promise?"

"I promise," Miranda replied with a smile. "Thank you. Did I ever just say thank you for all you and Sam have done for me over the years?"

"Twice a week, at least." Joan laughed, and then she sobered. "He's a tiger, that man," she added, nodding toward Harden, who was standing with his brothers and Sam. "Are you sure?"

"I love him," Miranda said simply.

Joan nodded. "Then it will be all right."

But would it, Miranda wondered, when Harden didn't love her.

"What a bunch," Sam said with a grin as he joined them. He put an affectionate arm around his sister. "At least you're no stranger to horses and ranch life," he said. "You'll fit right in here. Happy, kitten?"

"So happy," she assured him with a hug.

"Well, Harden will take care of you," he said. "No doubt about that. But," he added with a level stare, "no more leaping on horses' backs. I'm not sure your new husband's nerves will take it!"

She laughed, delighted that Harden had shared that incident with Sam. It meant that he liked her, anyway. He wanted her, too, and she was nervous despite the intimacy they'd shared. She didn't know if she was going to be enough for him.

Evan added his congratulations, along with the rest of the family. Theodora hugged her warmly and then looked with bitter hopelessness at Harden, who'd hardly spoken to her.

"He'll get over it one day," Miranda said hesitantly.

"Over the facts of his birth, maybe. Over Anita? I don't think he ever will," she added absently, oblivious to the shaken, tragic look that flashed briefly over Miranda's features before she quickly composed them.

Suddenly aware of what she'd said, Theodora turned, flushing. "I can't ever seem to say the right thing, can I?" she asked miserably. "I'm sorry, Miranda, I didn't mean that the way it sounded."

"You don't need to apologize to me," she told the older woman quietly. "I know he doesn't love me. It's all right. I'll try to be a good wife, and there will be children."

Theodora grimaced. Harden joined them, gathering Miranda with easy possessiveness under his arm to kiss her warmly.

"Hello, Mrs. Tremayne," he said softly. "How goes it?"

"I'm fine. How about you?" she asked.

"I'll be better when we get the reception out of the way. I had no idea we were related to so many people,'' he chuckled. Then he glanced at Theodora, and the laughter faded. "Few of them are related to me, of course," he added cuttingly.

Theodora didn't react. Her sad eyes searched his. "Have a nice honeymoon, Harden. You, too, Miranda." She turned and walked away, ignoring her son's hostility.

Miranda looked up at him worriedly. "You can't keep this up. You're cutting her to pieces."

His eyes narrowed. "Don't interfere," he cautioned quietly. "Theodora is my business."

"I'm your wife," she began.

"Yes. But that doesn't make you my conscience. Let's get this over with." He took her arm and led her into the house, where the caterers were ready for the reception.

The reception was held at the ranch, but Theodora ran interference long enough for the newlyweds to get away.

Connal and Pepi showed up for the wedding, and Miranda found that she and Pepi were fast becoming friends. Connal reminded her a lot of Evan, except that he was leaner and younger. Pepi was an elf, a gentle creature with big eyes. She and Connal had little Jamie Ben Tremayne with them, and he warmed Miranda's heart as he had the night they'd had supper with the rest of the family. But he made her ache for the child she'd lost. That, along with Theodora's faux pas put the only dampers on the day for her, and she carried the faint sadness along on their honeymoon.

They'd decided that Cancun was the best place to go, because they both had a passion for archaeology, and some Mayan ruins were near the hotel they'd booked into. Now, as her memories came back to haunt her, she wished again that she'd waited just a little longer, that she hadn't let Harden coax her into marriage so quickly.

What was done was done, though, and she had to make the best of it.

Harden had watched the joy go out of Miranda at the wedding, and he guessed that it was because of Connal and Pepi's baby. He almost groaned out loud. He should have carried her off and eloped, as he'd threatened. Now it was too late, and she was buried in the grief of the past. As if to emphasize the somber mood that had invaded what should have been a happy time, it began to pour rain.

Chapter Ten

Miranda hesitated in the doorway of their hotel room. It really hadn't occurred to her that they'd be given anything except a room with double beds. But there, dominating the room with its ocean view, was a huge king-size bed.

"We're married," Harden said curtly.

"Yes, of course." She stood aside to let the bellboy bring the luggage in and waited while Harden tipped him and closed the door.

She walked out onto the balcony and looked out over the Gulf of Mexico, all too aware of Harden behind her. She remembered the night at the bridge, and the way he'd rushed to save her. Presumably her action—rather, what he perceived to be a suicide attempt—had brought back unbearable memories for him. Suicide was something he knew all too much about, because the love of his life had died that way. Was it all because of Anita? Was he reliving the affair in his mind, and substituting Miranda? Except this time there was no suicide, there was a marriage and a happy ending. She could have cried.

Harden misattributed her silent brooding to her own bitter memories, so he didn't say anything. He stood beside her, letting the sea air ruffle his hair while he watched people on the beach and sea gulls making dives out of the sky.

He was still wearing the gray suit he'd been married in, and Miranda was wearing a dressy, oyster-colored suit of her own with a pale blue blouse. Her hair, in a chignon, was elegant and sleek. She looked much more like a businesswoman than a bride, a fact that struck Harden forcibly.

"Want to change?" he asked. "We could go swimming or just lay on the beach."

"Yes," she replied. Without looking at him, she opened her suitcase on its rack and drew out a conservative blue one-piece bathing suit and a simple white cover-up.

"I'll change in the bathroom," he said tersely, carrying his white trunks in there and closing the door firmly behind him.

It wasn't, Miranda thought wistfully, the most idyllic start for a honeymoon. She couldn't help remembering that Tim had been wild to get her into bed, though, and how unpleasant and embarrassing it had been for her, in broad daylight. Tim had been selfish and quick, and her memories of her wedding day were bitter.

Harden came back in just as she was gathering up her suntan lotion and dark glasses. In swimming trunks, he was everything Tim hadn't been. She paused with her hand in her suitcase and just stared, taking in the powerful, hair-roughened length of his body, tapering from broad, bronzed shoulders down a heavily muscled chest and stomach to lean hips and long legs. A male model, she thought, should look half as good.

He lifted an eyebrow, trying not to look as self-conscious as that appraisal made him feel. Not that he minded the pure pleasure on her face as she studied him, but it was beginning to have a noticeable effect on his body.

He turned. "Ready to go?" He didn't dare look too long at her in that clingy suit.

She picked up the sunglasses she'd been reaching for. "Yes. Should we take a towel?"

"They'll have them on the beach. If they don't, we'll buy a couple in that drugstore next to the lobby."

She followed him out to the beach. There was a buggy with fresh towels in it, being handed out to hotel patrons as they headed for the small palm umbrellas that dotted the white sand beach.

"The water is the most gorgeous color," she sighed, stretching out on a convenient lounger with her towel under her.

"Part of the attraction," he agreed. He stretched lazily and closed his eyes. "God, I'm tired. Are you?"

"Just a little. Of course, I'm just a young thing myself. Old people like you probably feel the— oh!"

She laughed as he tumbled her off the lounger onto the sand and pinned her there, his twinkling eyes just above her own. "Old, my foot," he murmured. His gaze fell to her mouth and lingered.

"You can't," she whispered. "It's a public beach."

"Yes, I can," he whispered back, and brought his mouth down over hers.

It was a long, sweet kiss. He drew back finally, his pale eyes quiet and curious on her relaxed face. "You were disturbed when we left the house. Did Theodora say something to you?"

She hesitated. Perhaps it would be as well to get it out into the open, she considered. "Harden," she began, her eyes hesitant as they met his, "Theodora told me about Anita."

His face froze. His eyes seemed to go blank. He lifted himself away from Miranda, and his expression gave away nothing of what he was feeling. Damn Theodora! Damn her for doing that to him, for stabbing him in the back! She had no right to drag up that tragedy on his wedding day. He'd spent years trying to forget; now Miranda was going to remind him of it and bring the anguish back.

He sat down on his lounger and lit a cigarette, leaning back to smoke it and watch the sea. "I suppose it's just as well that you know," he said finally. "But I won't talk about it. You understand?"

"Shutting me out again, Harden?" she asked sadly. "Is our marriage going to be like that, each of us with locked rooms in our hearts where the other can't come?"

"I won't talk about Anita, or about Theodora," he replied evenly. "Make what you like of it." He put on his own sunglasses and closed his eyes, effectively cutting off any further efforts at conversation.

Miranda was shattered. She knew then that she'd made another bad marriage, another big mistake, but it was too late to do anything about it. Now she had to live with it.

They had a quiet supper in the hotel restaurant much later. Harden was quiet, so was she. Conversation had been held to a minimum ever since they'd been on the beach, and Miranda's sad face was revealing her innermost thoughts.

When they got back to their room, Miranda turned and faced her husband with an expression that almost drove him to a furious outburst. It was so filled with bitter resignation, with determination to perform her wifely duties with stoic courage, that he could have turned the air blue.

"I want a drink," he said icily. "By the time I get back, you should be asleep and safe from any lecherous intentions I might have left. Good night, Mrs. Tremayne," he added contemptuously.

Miranda glared at him. "Thank you for a perfect day," she replied with equal contempt. "If I ever had any doubts about making our marriage work, you've sure set them to rest."

His eyes narrowed and glittered. "Is that a subtle hint that you want me, after all? In that case, let me oblige you."

He moved forward and picked her up unexpectedly, tossing her into the center of the huge bed. He followed her down, covering her with his own body, and unerringly finding her soft mouth with his own.

But she was too hurt to respond, too afraid of what he meant to do. It was like Tim...

She said Tim's name with real fear and Harden's head jerked up, his eyes glazing.

"You're just like him, really aren't you?" she choked, her eyes filled with bitter tears. "What you want, when you want it, always your way, no matter what the cost to anyone else."

He scowled. She looked so wounded, so alone. He reached down and touched her face, lightly, tracing the hot tears.

"I wouldn't hurt you," he said hesitantly. "Not that way."

"Go ahead, if you want to," she said tiredly, closing her eyes. "I don't care. I know better than to expect love from a man who can't forgive his mother a twelve-year-old tragedy or even the circumstances of his birth. Your mother must have loved your father very much to have risked the shame and humiliation of being pregnant with another man's child at the same time she was married to your stepfather." She opened her eyes, staring up at him. "But you don't know how to love, do you, Harden? Not anymore. All you knew of love is buried with your Anita. There's nothing left in here." She put her hand against his broad chest, where his heart was beating hard and raggedly. "Nothing at all. Only hate."

He jerked back from her hand and got to his feet, glaring down at her.

"Why did you marry me?" she asked sadly, sitting up to stare at him. "Was it pity, or just desire?"

He couldn't answer her. In the beginning, it had been pity. Desire came quickly after that, until she obsessed him. But since she'd been at the ranch, he'd had other feelings, feelings he'd never experienced even with Anita. His hand went to his chest where she'd touched it, absently rubbing the place her hand had rested, as if he could feel the warm imprint.

"You love me, don't you?" he asked unexpectedly.

She flushed, averting her eyes. "Think what you like."

He didn't know what to say, what to do, anymore. It had all seemed so simple. They'd get married and he'd make love to her whenever he liked, and they'd have children. Now it was much more complicated. He remembered the day she'd gone riding, and how black his world had gone until she'd come back. He remembered the terror, the sick fear, and suddenly he knew why. Knew everything.

"Listen," he began quietly. "This has all gone wrong. I think it might be a good idea—"

"If we break it off now?" she concluded mistakenly, her gray eyes staring bravely into his. "Yes, I think you're right. Neither of us is really ready for this kind of commitment yet. You were right when you said it was too soon."

"It isn't that," he said heavily. "And we can't get a divorce on our wedding day."

She gnawed her lower lip. "No. I guess not."

"We'll stay for a couple of days, at least. When we're home...we'll make decisions." He turned, picked up his clothes, and went into the bathroom to dress.

She changed quickly into a simple long cotton gown and got under the covers. She closed her eyes, but she needn't have bothered, because he didn't even look at her as he went out the door.

The rest of their stay in Cancun went by quickly, with the two of them being polite to each other and not much more. They went on a day trip to the ruins at Chichen Itza, wandering around the sprawling Maya ruins with scores of other tourists. The ruins covered four miles, with their widely spread buildings proving that it was a cult center and not just a conventional city. A huge plaza opened out to various religious buildings. The Mayan farmers would journey there for the year's great religious festivals; archaeologists also assumed that markets and council meetings drew the citizens to Chichen Itza.

The two most interesting aspects of the ancient city to Miranda were the observatory and the Sacred Cenote—or sacrificial well.

She stood at its edge and looked down past the underbrush into the murky water and shivered. It was nothing like the mental picture she had, of some small well-like structure. It was a cavernous opening that led down, down into the water, where over a period of many years, an estimated one hundred human beings were sacrificed to appease the gods in time of drought. The pool covered almost an acre, and it was sixty-five feet from its tree-lined edge down limestone cliffs to the water below.

"It gives me the screaming willies," a man beside Miranda remarked. "Imagine all those thousands of virgins being pushed off the cliff into that yucky water. Sacrificing people because of religion. Is that primitive, or what?"

"Ever hear of the Christians and the lions?" Harden drawled.

The man gave him a look and disappeared into the crowd.

If things had been less strained, Miranda might have corrected that assumption about the numbers, and sex, of the sacrificed Mayans and reminded the tourist that fact and fiction blended in this ancient place. But Harden had inhibited her too much. Sharing her long-standing education in the past of Chichen Itza probably wouldn't have endeared her to the tourist, either. Historical fact had been submerged in favor of Hollywood fiction in so many of the world's places of interest.

Miranda wandered back onto the grassy plaza and stared at the observatory. She knew that despite their infrequent sacrificial urges, the Maya were an intelligent people who had an advanced concept of astronomy and mathematics, and a library that covered the entire history of Maya. Sadly Spanish missionaries in 1545 burned the books that contained the Maya history. Only three survived to the present day.

Miranda wandered back to the bus. It was a sobering experience to look at the ruins and consider that in 500 B.C. this was a thriving city, where people lived

and worshiped and probably never considered that
their civilization would ever end. Just like us, she
thought philosophically, and shivered. Just like my
marriages, both in ruins, both like Chichen Itza.

She was somber back to the hotel, and for the rest
of their stay in Cancun. She did things mechanically,
and without any real enjoyment. Not that Harden was
any more jovial than she was. Probably, she considered, he'd decided that there wasn't much to salvage
from their brief relationship. And maybe it was just as
well.

When they got back to Jacobsville, Theodora insisted that they stay with her until their own home was
ready for occupancy—a matter of barely a week.
Neither of them had the heart to announce that their
honeymoon had resulted in a coming divorce.

Evan, however, sensed that something was wrong.
Their first evening back, he steered Miranda onto the
front porch with a determined expression on his
swarthy face.

"Okay. What's wrong?" he asked abruptly.

She was taken aback at the sudden question. "W-
what?"

"You heard me," he replied. "You both came home
looking like death warmed over, and if anything except arguing took place during the whole trip, I'll eat
my hat."

"The one that could double as an umbrella?" she
asked with a feeble attempt at humor.

"Cut it out. I know Harden. What happened?"

Miranda sighed, giving in. "He's still in love with Anita, that's all, so we decided that we made a mistake and we're going to get it annulled."

He raised an eyebrow. "Annulled?" he emphasized.

She colored. "Yes, well, for a man who seemed to be bristling with desire, he sure changed."

"You do know that he's a virgin?" Evan asked.

She knew her jaw was gaping. She closed her mouth. "He's a what?"

"You didn't know," he murmured. "Well, he'd kill me for telling you, but it's been family gossip for years. He wanted to be a minister, and he's had nothing to do with women since Anita died. A ladies' man, he ain't."

Miranda knew that, but she'd assumed he had some experience. He acted as if he had.

"Are you sure?" she blurted out.

"Of course I'm sure. Look, he's backward and full of hang-ups. It's going to be up to you to make the first move, or you'll end up in divorce court before you know it."

"But, I can't," she groaned.

"Yes, you can. You're a woman. Get some sexy clothes and drive him nuts. Wear perfume, drop handkerchiefs, vamp him. Then get him behind a locked door and let nature take its course. For God's sake, woman, you can't give up on him less than a week after the wedding!"

"He doesn't love me!"

"Make him," he said, his eyes steely and level. "And don't tell me you can't. I saw him when you were late getting back on that killer stallion. I've never seen him so shaken. A man who can feel that kind of fear for a woman can love her."

She hesitated now, lured by the prospect of Harden falling in love with her. "Do you really think he could?"

He smiled. "He isn't as cold as he likes people to think he is. There's a soft core in that man that's been stomped on too many times."

"I guess I could try," she said slowly.

"I guess you could."

She smiled and went back inside, her mind whirling with possibilities.

The next day, Miranda asked Theodora to take her shopping, and she bought the kind of clothes she'd never worn in her life. She had her hair trimmed and styled, and she bought underwear that made her blush.

"Is this a campaign?" Theodora asked on the way home, her dark eyes twinkling.

"I guess it is," she sighed. "Right now, it looks as if he's ready to toss me back into the lake."

"I'm sorry that I mentioned Anita on your wedding day," the older woman said heavily. "I could see the light go out of you. Harden and I may never make our peace, Miranda, but I never meant to put you in the middle."

"I know that." She turned in the seat, readjusting her seat belt. "Does Harden know anything about his real father?"

Theodora smiled. "No. He's never wanted to."

"Would you tell me?"

The older woman's eyes grew misty with remembrance. "He was a captain in the Green Berets, actually," she said. "I met him at a Fourth of July parade, of all things, in Houston while my husband and I were temporarily separated. He was a farm boy from Tennessee, but he had a big heart and he was full of fun. We went everywhere together. He spoiled me, pampered me, fell in love with me. Before I knew it, I was in love with him, desperately in love with him!"

She turned onto the road that led to the ranch, frowning now while Miranda listened, entranced. "Neither of us wanted an affair, but what we felt was much too explosive to... Well, I guess you know about that," she added shyly. "People in love have a hard time controlling their passions. We were no different. He gave me a ring, a beautiful emerald-and-diamond ring that had been his mother's, and I filed for divorce. We were going to be married as soon as the divorce was final. But he was sent to Vietnam and the first day there, the Viet Cong attacked and he was killed by mortar fire."

"And you discovered you were pregnant," Miranda prompted when the other woman hesitated, her eyes anguished.

"Yes." She shifted behind the wheel. "Abortion was out of the question. I loved Barry so much, more than my own life. I'd have risked anything to have his child. I didn't know what to do. I got sick and couldn't work, and I had nowhere to go when I was asked to leave my apartment for nonpayment of rent. About that time, Jesse, my own husband, came and asked me to come back to the ranch, to end the separation. Evan was very young, and he had a governess for him, but he missed me.''

"Did your husband love you?'' Miranda asked softly.

"Yes. That made it so much worse, you see, because he was jealous and overpossessive and overprotective—that's why I left him in the first place. But perhaps the experience taught him something, because he never threw the affair up to me. He brought me back home and after the first few weeks, he became involved with my pregnancy. He loved children, you know. It didn't even matter to him that Harden wasn't his own. He never let it matter to anyone else, either. We had a good life. I did my grieving for Barry in secret, and then I fell in love with my husband all over again. But Harden has made sure since Anita's death that I paid for all my old sins. Interesting, that the instrument of my punishment for an illicit affair and an illegitimate child is the child himself.''

"I'm sorry,'' Miranda said. "It can't be easy for you.''

"It isn't easy for Harden, either,'' came the surprising reply. Theodora smiled sadly as they reached the house. "That gets me through it.'' She looked at Miranda with dark, somber eyes. "He's the image of Barry.''

"I wish you could make him listen.''

"What's the old saying, 'if wishes were horses, beggars could ride'?'' Theodora shook her head. "My dear, we're all walking these days.''

Later, like a huntress waiting for her prey to appear, Miranda donned the sexy underwear and the incredibly see-through lemon-yellow gown she'd bought, sprayed herself with perfume, and exhibited herself in a seductive position on the bed in the bedroom they'd been sharing. Harden made sure he didn't come in until she was asleep, and he was gone before she woke in the morning. But tonight, she was waiting for him. If what Evan said, as incredible as it seemed, was true, and Harden was innocent, it was going to be delicious to seduce him. She had to make allowances for his pride, of course, so she couldn't admit that she knew. That made it all the more exciting.

It was a long time before the door swung open and her tired, dust-stained husband came in the door. He paused with his Stetson in his hand and gaped at her where she lay on the bed, on her side, one perfect small breast almost bare.

"Hi, cowboy," she said huskily, and smiled at him. "Long day?"

"What the hell are you dudded up for?" he asked curtly.

She eased off the bed and stood up, so that he could get a good view of her creamy body under the gauzy fabric of her gown. She stretched, lifting her breasts so that the already hard tips were pushing against the bodice.

"I bought some new clothes, that's all," she murmured drowsily. "Going to have a shower?"

He muttered something under his breath about having one with ice cubes and slammed the bathroom door behind him.

Miranda laughed softly to herself when she heard the shower running. Now if only she could keep her nerve, if only she could dull his senses so that he couldn't resist her. She pulled the hem of the gown up to her thighs and the strap off one rounded shoulder and lay against the pillows, waiting.

He came out, eventually, with a dark green towel secured around his hips. She looked up at him, her eyes slitted, her lips parted invitingly while his eyes slid over her body with anything but a shy, innocent appraisal. The look was so hot, she writhed under it.

"Is this what it took for your late husband?" he asked, his own eyes narrow and almost insulting. "Did you have to dress up to get him interested?"

Her breath caught. She sat up, righting her gown. "Harden..." she began, ready to explain, despite her intention not to.

"Well, I don't need that kind of stimulation when I'm interested," he said, controlling a fiercely subdued rage over her behavior. She must think him impotent, at the least, to go so far to get him into bed. Which only made him more suspicious about her motives.

"You used to be interested," she stammered.

"So I did, before you decided that I needed reforming, before you started interfering in my life. I wanted you. But not anymore, honey, and all those cute tricks you're practicing don't do a damned thing for me."

He pulled her against him, "Can't you tell?"

His lack of interest was so blatant that she turned her eyes away, barely aware that he was pulling clothes out of drawers and closets. Tears blinded her. She hid under the covers and pulled them up to her blushing face, shivering with shame. This had been Tim's favorite weapon, making her feel inadequate, too little a woman to arouse him. Her pride lay on the floor at Harden's feet, and he didn't even care.

"For future reference, I'll do the chasing when I'm interested in sex," he said, glaring down at her white face. "I don't want it with you, not anymore. I told you it was over. You should have listened."

"Yes. I should have," she said hoarsely.

He felt wounded all over. She'd loved him, he knew she had, but she couldn't just be his wife, she had to be a reformer, to harp on his feud with Theodora, to make him seem cruel and selfish. He'd been stinging ever since Cancun, especially since some of those accusations were right on the money. But this was the last straw, this seductive act of hers. He'd had women come on to him all his adult life, their very aggressiveness turning him off. He hadn't expected his own wife to treat him like some casual stud to satisfy her passions. Was she really that desperate for sex?

He turned and went out of the room. It didn't help that he could hear Miranda crying even through the closed door.

Evan heard it, too, and minutes later he confronted his brother in the barn, where Harden was checking on one of the mares in foal.

The bigger man was taking off his hat as he walked down the wide, wood-chip-shaving-filled aisle between the rows of stalls, his swarthy face set in hard lines, his mouth barely visible as his jaw clenched.

"That does it," he said, and kept coming. "That really does it. That poor woman's had enough from you!"

Harden threw off his own hat and stood, waiting. "Go ahead, throw a punch. You'll get it back, with interest," he replied, his tone lazy, his blue eyes bright with anger.

"She goes shopping and buys all sorts of sexy clothes to turn you on, and then you leave her in tears! Doesn't it matter to you that she was trying to make it easy for you?" he demanded.

Harden frowned. Something wasn't right here. "Easy for me?" he prompted.

Evan sighed angrily. "I wasn't going to tell you, but maybe I'd better. I told her the truth about you," he said shortly.

"About what?"

"You know about what!" Evan growled. "It was her right to know, after all, she's your wife."

"What did you tell her, for God's sake?" Harden raged, at the end of his patience.

"The truth." Evan squared his shoulders and waited for the explosion as he replied, "I told her you were a virgin."

Chapter Eleven

For a minute Harden just stood staring at his brother, looking as if he hadn't heard a word. Then he began to laugh, softly at first, building into a roar of sound that echoed down the long aisle.

"It isn't funny," Evan glowered at him. "My God, it's nothing to be ashamed of. There are plenty of men who are celibate. Priests, for instance..."

Harden laughed louder.

Evan wiped his sleeve across his broad, damp forehead and sighed heavily. "What's so damned funny?"

Harden stopped to get his breath before he answered, and lit a cigarette. He took a deep draw, staring amusedly at his older brother.

"I never bothered to deny it, because it didn't matter. But I ought to deck you for passing that old gossip on to Miranda. I gave her hell upstairs for what she did. I had no idea she was supposed to be helping me through my first time!''

Evan cocked his head, narrowing one eye. ''You aren't a virgin?''

Harden didn't answer him. He lifted the cigarette to his mouth. ''Is that why she went on that spending spree in town, to buy sexy clothes to vamp me with?''

''Yes. I'm as much help as Mother, I guess,'' Evan said quietly. ''I overheard her telling Miranda that you'd never get over Anita.''

Harden frowned. ''When?''

''At the reception, before you left on your honeymoon.''

Harden groaned and closed his eyes. He turned to the barn wall and hit it soundly with his fist. ''Damn the luck!''

''One misunderstanding after another, isn't it?'' Evan leaned a broad shoulder against the wall. ''Was she right? Are you still in love with Anita?''

''No. Maybe you were right about that. Maybe it was her time, and Mother was just a link in the chain of events.''

''My God,'' Evan exclaimed reverently. ''Is that really you talking, or do you just have a fever?'' he asked dryly.

Harden glanced up at the lighted window of the room he shared with Miranda. ''I've got a fever, all right. And I know just how to get it down.''

He left Evan standing and went up to the bedroom, his eyes gleaming with mischief and anticipated pleasure.

But the sight that met him when he opened the door wasn't conducive to pleasure. Miranda was fully dressed in a pretty white silk dress that was even more seductive than the nightgown she'd discarded, and she was packing a suitcase.

She turned a tearstained face to his. "Don't worry, I'm going," she said shortly. "You don't have to throw me off the place."

He closed the door calmly, turned the lock, and tossed his hat onto a chair before he moved toward her.

"You can stop right there," she said warningly. "I'm going home!"

"You are home," he said evenly.

He swept the suitcase, clothes and all, off the bed onto the floor into a littered heap and bent to lift a startled Miranda in his hard arms.

"You put me down!" she raged.

"Anything to oblige, sweetheart." He threw her onto the bed and before she could roll away, he had her pinned against the disheveled covers, one long leg holding her thrashing body. She fought him like a tigress until he caught her wrists and pressed them into the mattress on either side of her head.

Her hair was a dark cloud around her flushed face as she stared up at him furiously, her silver eyes flashing at him.

"I've had enough of damned men!" she raged at him. "It was bad enough having Tim tell me I wasn't woman enough to hold a man without having you rub my face in it, too! I have my pride!"

"Pride, and a lot of other faults," he mused. "Bad temper, impatience, interfering in things that don't concern you..."

"What are you, Mr. Sweetness and Light, a pattern for perfect manhood?!"

"Not by a long shot," he said pleasantly, studying her face. "You're a wildcat, Miranda. Everything I ever wanted, even if it did take me a long time to realize it, and to admit it."

"You don't want me," she said, her voice breaking as she tried to speak bravely about it. "You showed me...!"

"I had a cold shower, remember," he whispered, smiling gently. "Here. Feel."

He moved slowly, sensuously, and something predictable and beautiful happened to him, something so blatant that she caught her breath.

"I want you," he said softly. "But it's much, much more than wanting. Do you like poetry, Miranda?" he breathed at her lips, brushing them with maddening leisure as he spoke. "'Shall I compare thee to a summer's day? Thou art more lovely, and more temperate...'" He kissed her slowly, nibbling at her lower lip while she trembled with pleasure. "Shakespeare couldn't have been talking about you, could he, sweetheart? You aren't temperate, even if you are every bit as lovely as a summer's day...!"

The kiss grew rough, and deep, and his lean hands found her hips, grinding them up against his fierce arousal.

"This is how much I want you," he bit off at her lips. "I hope you took vitamins, because you're going to need every bit of strength you've got."

She couldn't even speak. His hands were against her skin, and then his mouth was. She'd never in her wildest dreams imagined some of the ways he touched her, some of the things he whispered while he aroused her. He took her almost effortlessly to a fever pitch of passion and then calmed her and started all over again.

It was the sweetest kind of pleasure to feel him get the fabric away from her hot skin, and then to feel his own hair-roughened body intimately against her own. It was all of heaven to kiss and be kissed, to touch and be touched, to let him pleasure her until she was mindless with need.

"Evan said...you were...a virgin," she whispered, her voice breaking as she looked, shocked, into the amused indulgence of his face when the tension was unbearable.

He laughed, the sound soft and predatory. "Am I?" he whispered, and pushed down, hard.

She couldn't believe what she was feeling. His face blurred and then vanished, and it was all feverish motion and frantic grasping and sharp, hot pleasure that brought convulsive statisfaction.

She lay in his arms afterward, tears running helplessly down her cheeks while he smoked a cigarette and absently smoothed her disheveled hair. She was still trembling in the aftermath.

"Are you all right, little one?" he asked gently.

"Yes." She laid her wet cheek against his shoulder. "I didn't know," she stammered.

"It's different, every time," he replied quietly. "But sometimes there's a level of pleasure that you can only experience with one certain person." His lips brushed her forehead with breathless tenderness. "It helps if you're in love with them."

"I suppose you couldn't help but know that," she said, her eyes faintly sad. "I always did wear my heart on my sleeve."

He nuzzled her face until she lifted it to his quiet, vivid blue eyes. "I love you," he said quietly. "Didn't you know?"

No, she didn't know. Her breath stopped in her throat and she felt the flush that even reddened her breasts.

"My God," he murmured, watching it spread. "I've never seen a woman blush here." He touched her breasts, very gently.

"Well, now you have, and you can stop throwing your conquests in my face— Oh!"

His mouth stopped the tirade, and he smiled against it. "They weren't conquests, they were educational experiences that made me the perfect specimen of male prowess you see before you."

"Of all the conceited people . . ." she began.

He touched her, and she gasped, clinging to him. "What was that bit, about being conceited?" he asked.

She moaned and curled into his body, shivering. "Harden!" she cried.

"I'll bet you didn't even know that only one man out of twenty is capable of this. . . ."

The cigarette went into the ashtray and his body covered hers. And he gave her a long and unbearably sweet lesson in rare male endurance that lasted almost until morning.

When she woke, he was dressed, whistling to himself as he whipped a belt around his lean hips and secured the big silver buckle.

"Awake?" he murmured dryly. He arched an eyebrow as she moved and groaned and winced. "I could stay home and we could make love some more."

She caught her breath, gaping at him. "And your brother thinks you're a virgin!" she burst out.

He shrugged. "We all make mistakes."

"Yes, well the people who write sex manuals could do two chapters on you!" she gasped.

He grinned. "I could return the compliment. Don't get up unless you want to. Having you take to your bed can only reflect favorably on my reputation in the household."

She burst out laughing at the expression on his face. She sat up, letting the covers fall below her bare breasts, and held out her arms.

He dropped into them, kissing her with lazy affection. "I love you," he whispered. "I'm sorry if I was a little too enthusiastic about showing it."

"No more enthusiastic than I was," she murmured softly. She reached up and kissed him back. "I wish you could stay home. I wish I wasn't so... incapacitated."

"Don't sound regretful," he chuckled. "Wasn't it fun getting you that way?"

She clung to him, sighing. "Oh, yes." Her eyes opened and she stared past him at the wall, almost purring as his hands found her silky breasts and caressed them softly. "Harden?"

"What, sweetheart?"

She closed her eyes. "Nothing. Just...I love you."

He smiled, and reached down to kiss her again.

When he went downstairs to have Jeanie May take a tray up to Miranda, Evan grinned like a Cheshire cat.

"Worn her out after only one day? You'd better put some vitamins on that tray and feed her up," he said.

Harden actually grinned back. "I'm working on that."

"I gather everything's going to be all right?"

"No thanks to you," Harden said meaningfully.

Evan's cheeks went ruddy. "I was only trying to help, and how was I to know the truth? My God, you never went around with women, you never brought anybody home... You *could* have been a virgin!"

Harden smiled secretly. "Yes, I could have."

The way he put it made Evan more suspicious than ever. "Are you?" he asked.

"Not anymore," came the dry reply. "Even if I was," he added to further confound the older man. The smile faded. "Where's Theodora?"

"Out feeding her chickens."

He nodded, and went out the back door. He'd said some hard things to Theodora over the years, and Miranda was right about his vendetta. It was time to run up the white flag.

Theodora saw him coming and grimaced, and when he saw that expression, something twisted in his heart.

"Good morning," he said, his hands stuffed into his pockets.

Theodora glanced at him warily. "Good morning," she replied, tossing corn to her small congregation of Rhode Island Reds.

"I thought we might have a talk."

"Why bother?" she asked quietly. "You and Miranda will be in your own place by next week. You won't have to come over here except at Christmas."

He took out a cigarette and lit it, trying to decide how to proceed. It wasn't going to be easy. In all fairness, it shouldn't be, he conceded.

"I...would like to know about my father," he said.

The bowl slid involuntarily from Theodora's hands and scattered the rest of the corn while she stared, white-faced, at Harden. "What?" she asked.

"I want to know about my father," he said tersely. "Who he was, what he looked like." He hesitated. "How you...felt about him."

"I imagine you know that already," she replied proudly. "Don't you?"

He blew out a cloud of smoke. "Yes. I think I do, now," he agreed. "There's a big difference between love and infatuation. I didn't know, until I met Miranda."

"All the same, I'm sorry about Anita," she said tightly. "I've had to live with it, too, you know."

"Yes." He hesitated. "It...must have been hard for you. Having me, living here." He stared at her, searching for words. "If Miranda and I hadn't married, if I'd given her a child, I know she'd have had it. Cherished it. Loved it, because it would have been a part of me."

Theodora nodded.

"And all the shame, all the taunts and cutting remarks, would have passed right off her because we loved each other so much," he continued. "She'd have raised my child, and what she felt for him would have been . . . special, because a love like that only happens once for most people."

Theodora averted her eyes, blinded by tears. "If they're lucky," she said huskily.

"I didn't know," he said unsteadily, unconsciously repeating the very words Miranda had said to him the night before. "I never loved . . . until now."

Theodora couldn't find the words. She turned, finding an equal emotion in Harden's face. She stood there, small and defenseless, and something burst inside him.

He held out his arms. Theodora went into them, crying her heart out against his broad chest, washing away all the bitterness and pain and hurt. She felt something wet against her cheek, where his face rested, and around them the wind blew.

"Mother," he said huskily.

Her thin arms tightened, and she smiled, thanking God for miracles.

Later, they sat on the front porch and she told him about his father, bringing out a long-hidden album that contained the only precious photographs she had.

"He looks like me," Harden mused, seeing his own face reflected in what, in the photograph, was a much younger one.

"He was like you," she replied. "Brave and loyal and loving. He never shirked his duty, and I loved him with all my heart. I still do. I always will."

"Did your husband know how you felt?"

"Oh, yes," she said simply. "I was too honest to pretend. But he loved children, you see, and my pregnancy brought out all his protective instincts. He loved me the way I loved Barry," she added sadly. "I gave him all I could, and hoped that it would be enough." She brushed at a tear. "He loved you, you know. Even though you weren't blood kin to him, he was crazy about you from the day you were born."

He smiled. "Yes. I remember." He frowned as he looked at his mother. "I'm sorry. I'm so damned sorry."

"You had to find your way," she said. "It took a long time, and you had plenty of sorrow along the way. I knew what you were going through in school, with the other children throwing the facts of your birth up to you. But if I had interfered, I would have made it worse, don't you see? You had to learn to cope. Experience is always the best teacher."

"Even if it doesn't seem so at the time. Yes, I know that now."

"About Anita..."

He took her thin, wrinkled hand in his and held it tightly. "Anita's people would never have let us marry. But even now, I can't really be sure that it was me she wanted, or just someone her parents didn't approve of.

She was very young, and high-strung, and her mother died in an asylum. Evan said that if God wants someone to live, they will, despite the odds. I don't know why I never realized that until now."

She smiled gently. "I think Miranda's opened your eyes to a lot of things."

He nodded. "She won't ever forget her husband, or the child she lost. That's a good thing. Our experiences make us the people we are. But the past is just that. She and I will make our own happiness. And there'll be other babies. A lot of them, I hope."

"Oh, that reminds me! Jo Ann's pregnant!"

"Maybe it's the water," Harden said, and smiled at her.

She laughed. The smile faded and her eyes were eloquent. "I love you very much."

"I...love you," he said stiffly. He'd said it more in two days than he'd said it in his life. Probably it would get easier as he went along. Theodora didn't seem to mind, though. She just beamed and after a minute, she turned the page in the old album and started relating other stories about Harden's father.

It was late afternoon before Miranda came downstairs, and Evan was trying not to smile as she walked gingerly into the living room where he and Harden were discussing a new land purchase.

"Go ahead, laugh," she dared Evan. "It's all your fault!"

Evan did laugh. "I can't believe that's a complaint, judging by the disgustingly smug look on your husband's face," he mused.

She shook her head, as bright as a new penny as she went into Harden's arms and pressed close.

"No complaints at all," Harden said, sighing. He closed his eyes and laid his cheek against her dark hair. "I just hope I won't die of happiness."

"People have," Evan murmured. But his eyes were sad as he turned away from them. "Well, I'd better get busy. I should be back in time for supper, if this doesn't run late."

"Give Anna my love," Harden replied.

Evan grimaced. "Anna is precocious," he muttered. "Too forward and too outspoken by far for a nineteen-year-old."

"Most of my friends were married by that age," Miranda volunteered.

Evan looked uncomfortable and almost haunted for a minute. "She doesn't even need to be there," he said shortly. "Her mother and I can discuss a land deal without her."

"Is her mother pretty?" Miranda asked. "Maybe she's chaperoning you."

"Her mother is fifty and as thin as a rail," he replied. "Hardly my type."

"What does Anna look like?" Miranda asked, curious now.

"She's voluptuous, to coin a phrase," Harden answered for his taciturn brother. "Blonde and blue-eyed and tall. She's been swimming around Evan for four years, but he won't even give her a look. He's thirty-four, you know. Much too old for a mere child of nineteen."

"That's damned right," he told Harden forcibly. "A man doesn't rob cradles. My God, I've known her since she was a child." He frowned. "Which she still is, of course," he added quickly.

"Go ahead, convince yourself," Harden nodded.

"I don't have to do any convincing!"

"Have a good time."

"I'm going to be discussing land prices," he said, glaring at Harden.

"I used to enjoy that," Harden said, shrugging. "You might, too."

"That will be the day. I . . ."

"Harden, want a chocolate cake for supper?" Theodora called from the doorway, smiling.

Harden drew Miranda closer and smiled back. "Love one, if it's not too much trouble."

"No trouble at all," she said gently.

"Mother!" he called when she turned, and Evan's eyes popped.

"What?" Theodora asked pleasantly.

"Butter icing?"

She laughed. "That's just what I had in mind!"

Evan's jaw was even with his collar. "My God!" he exclaimed.

Harden looked at him. "Something wrong?"

"You called her Mother!"

"Of course I did, Evan, she's my mother," he replied.

"You've never called her anything except Theodora," Evan explained. "And you smiled at her. You even made sure she wouldn't be put to any extra work making you a cake.'' He looked at Miranda. ''Maybe he's sick.''

Miranda looked up at him shyly and blushed. ''No, I don't think so.''

''I'd have to be weak if I were sick,'' he explained to Evan, and Miranda made an embarrassed sound and hid her face against his shoulder.

Evan shook his head. ''Miracles,'' he said absently. He shrugged, smiling, and turned toward the door, reaching for his hat as he walked through the hall. ''I'll be back by supper.''

''Anna's a great cook,'' Harden reminded him. ''You might get invited for supper.''

''I won't accept. I told you, damn it, she's too young for me!''

He went out, slamming the door behind him.

Harden led Miranda out the front door and onto the porch, to share the swing with him. ''Anna wants to love him, but he won't let her,'' he explained.

''Why?''

''I'll tell you one dark night,'' he promised. ''But for now, we've got other things to think about. Haven't we?'' he added softly.

''Oh, yes.'' She caught her her breath just before he took it away, and she smiled under his hungry kiss.

The harsh memories of the wreck that had almost destroyed Miranda's life faded day by wonderful day, as Miranda and Harden grew closer. Theodora was drawn into the circle of their happiness and the new relationship she enjoyed with Harden lasted even when the newlyweds moved into their own house.

But Miranda's joy was complete weeks later, when she fainted at a family gathering and a white-faced Harden carried her hotfoot to the doctor.

"Nothing to worry about," Dr. Barnes assured them with a grin, after a cursory examination and a few pointed questions. "Nothing at all. A small growth that will come out all by itself—in just about seven months."

They didn't understand at first. And when they did, Miranda could have sworn that Harden's eyes were watery as he hugged her half to death in the doctor's office.

For Miranda, the circle was complete. The old life was a sad memory, and now there was a future of brightness and warmth to look forward to in a family circle that closed around her like gentle arms. She had, she considered as she looked up at her handsome husband, the whole world right here beside her.

*   *   *   *   *

WRITTEN IN THE STARS

Amorous Aries
Locks Horns With
Feisty Female Employee!

Read all about it in THANK YOUR LUCKY STARS by Lydia Lee in April . . . the fourth book in our WRITTEN IN THE STARS series!

Editor-in-chief Max Hunter was in charge of the newspaper, and the sexy, stubborn Aries wasn't about to let red-haired resident astrologer Jane Smith investigate anything but the stars—in his eyes!

Get the scoop on the Aries man in THANK YOUR LUCKY STARS by Lydia Lee in April . . . only from Silhouette Romance!

Available in April at your favorite retail outlet, or order your copy by sending your name, address, zip or postal code along with a check or money order for $2.50 (please do not send cash), plus 75¢ postage and handling ($1.00 in Canada), payable to Silhouette Reader Service to:

In the U.S.
3010 Walden Ave.,
Box 1396
Buffalo, NY 14269-1396

In Canada
P.O. Box 609,
Fort Erie, Ontario
L2A 5X3

Please specify book title with your order.
Canadian residents please add applicable federal and provincial taxes.   APRSTAR-1R

WRITTEN IN THE STARS

Will The Pisces Man Be Lured Into Romance?

Find out in March with FOR HEAVEN'S SAKE by Brenda Trent . . . the third book in our WRITTEN IN THE STARS series!

There was only one fish in the sea for pet groomer Kelly-Ann Keernan—she'd fallen for sexy Steve Jamison, hook, line and sinker! But will the private Pisces man ever say goodbye to bachelorhood and hello to married bliss?

Be sure to catch the passionate Pisces man's story, FOR HEAVEN'S SAKE by Brenda Trent . . . only from Silhouette Romance!

Available now at your favorite retail outlet, or order your copy by sending your name, address, zip or postal code along with a check or money order for $2.50 (please do not send cash), plus 75¢ postage and handling ($1.00 in Canada), payable to Silhouette Reader Service to:

In the U.S.	In Canada
3010 Walden Ave.,	P.O. Box 609,
Box 1396,	Fort Erie, Ontario
Buffalo, NY 14269-1396	L2A 5X3

Please specify book title with your order.
Canadian residents please add applicable federal and provincial taxes

MARSTAR-R

 Silhouette Books®